**Please check all items for damages
before leaving the Library.
Thereafter you will be held
responsible for all injuries
to items beyond reasonable wear.**

Helen M. Plum Memorial Library

Lombard, Illinois

A daily fine will be charged for
overdue materials.

SEP   2011

AWAY

Teri Hall

DIAL BOOKS
an imprint of Penguin Group (USA) Inc.

Y
FICTION
HAL

DIAL BOOKS
An imprint of Penguin Group (USA) Inc.
Published by The Penguin Group • Penguin Group (USA) Inc., 375 Hudson Street, New York, NY 10014, U.S.A.
Penguin Group (Canada), 90 Eglinton Avenue East, Suite 700, Toronto, Ontario, Canada M4P 2Y3 • (a division of
Pearson Penguin Canada Inc.) • Penguin Books Ltd, 80 Strand, London WC2R 0RL, England • Penguin Ireland, 25
St. Stephen's Green, Dublin 2, Ireland (a division of Penguin Books Ltd) • Penguin Group (Australia), 250 Camberwell
Road, Camberwell, Victoria 3124, Australia • (a division of Pearson Australia Group Pty Ltd) • Penguin Books India
Pvt Ltd, 11 Community Centre, Panchsheel Park, New Delhi - 110 017, India • Penguin Group (NZ), 67 Apollo Drive,
Rosedale, Auckland 0632, New Zealand • (a division of Pearson New Zealand Ltd) • Penguin Books (South Africa) (Pty)
Ltd, 24 Sturdee Avenue, Rosebank, Johannesburg 2196, South Africa • Penguin Books Ltd, Registered Offices: 80 Strand,
London WC2R 0RL, England

This is a work of fiction. All the names, characters, places, organizations, and events portrayed in this book
are products of the author's imagination or are used fictitiously to lend a sense of realism to the story.

Designed by Jennifer Kelly
Text set in Minion
Printed in the U.S.A.

10 9 8 7 6 5 4 3 2 1

Library of Congress Cataloging-in-Publication Data
Hall, Teri.
 Away / Teri Hall.
 p. cm.
 Sequel to: The Line.
 Summary: After helping heal Malgam, Rachel learns that her father is still living in the devastated territory of Away but
has been captured by another clan, who are planning to use him to make a deal with the government on the other side
of the Line, and she joins the daring rescue party that must risk much to save him.
 ISBN 978-0-8037-3502-6 (hardcover)
 [1. Science fiction. 2. Rescues—Fiction. 3. Survival—Fiction. 4. Government, Resistance to—Fiction.] I. Title.
 PZ7.H14874Aw 2011   [Fic]—dc22   2011001163

AWAY

CHAPTER 1

Awake, Rachel?" Pathik appeared, as he had for the last three mornings, holding two steaming cups of a bitter beverage the Others called root brew. He handed one to Rachel and sat down next to her. He looked weary, but he had looked that way for the whole of their short acquaintance.

She was *barely* awake, huddled on a crudely carved log that served as a bench, as close to the camp's central fire as she could get. During the six-day hike from the Line to Pathik's base camp, Rachel had begun to believe she would never be warm again. Though it was far from luxurious, the central fire pit had become one of her favorite places in camp.

She wrapped both hands around the dented metal cup and blew on the hot liquid, wishing for some kalitea, sweetened with sugar, served up in one of Ms. Moore's fine china cups. The cup she held now looked like it had been around for decades, yet it was one of the most modern things—at least of those still in one piece—that she had seen since she arrived Away. Everywhere she looked something mutely testified to the way time had just stopped here. The few buildings left standing were shells, with empty rooms and blown-out windows. There was no running water or heat. The lighting was provided by candles or oil. When the bombs went off all those years ago and Away was born, the activation of the Line cut off much more than a way back home for these people. It cut off any sort of access to technology. The forebears of the group that lived in this camp had had to figure out how to survive. Rachel was amazed they had managed it.

"Any change?" Rachel tried to read Pathik's expression for news of his father, Malgam. He was the reason she had Crossed the Line; he'd fallen ill and the camp healer couldn't help him. She'd helped Pathik bring medicine that the Others didn't have.

"Indigo said his fever broke last night. He's going to be okay, I think." Pathik spoke quietly; most of the camp's inhabitants were still sleeping.

Indigo was Pathik's grandfather, Malgam's father. Rachel had seen his face many times before she actually met him; Ms. Moore, the lady for whom Rachel's mother, Vivian, worked, had had a framed digim of him on her mantel. But the man in the digim was much younger looking, and his hair had been a rich brown color. Somehow, Rachel had expected Indigo to look just like the digim, though it had been taken many years ago. When she first saw him on the night they arrived in camp, she was shocked at how his brown hair was now all silvery gray.

His eyes were the same, though—an intense, bottomless blue. When Indigo had looked at her the evening they arrived in camp, when he had thanked her for bringing the antibiotics Malgam needed, she felt like his eyes saw *inside* her. His smile shone through the worry she could see in his face and made her feel like he approved of her somehow.

"Do you know where my father is?" she had asked. She hadn't been able to help it, though she knew she should wait, knew that he needed to focus on his son.

"Your father?" He had tilted his head down at her, confused.

"She has a digim of Daniel." Pathik had whispered the words so the rest of the group gathered around the fire that night couldn't hear. "She showed it to me." He lowered his voice even more. "She says he's her father."

Indigo's eyes had widened then, but he hadn't answered her question.

"We will talk," he had said gently, "later." He had rushed away then, to tend to his son, but something lingered in her, some sense that he was an ally. It was a comforting balm in the midst of the confusion of that night—her first night in the Others' camp. She hadn't spoken to him again since then. She'd been waiting, catching glimpses of him as he went to tend to Malgam, but there had been no opportunity to speak to him.

"Morning, Jab." Pathik's voice brought Rachel back to the present, back to the chilly morning air and the smoke tendrilling toward her face. She looked up and saw Jab, one of the Others who had been with Pathik when he made his trek to the Line in search of medicine. He was holding his own cup of root brew, shivering.

"Have a seat." Pathik patted the log next to him. Jab glanced at Rachel and sat down.

"Morning," said Jab. He stared straight ahead at the fire.

Rachel was glad Pathik sat between them, though she knew that would provide no protection if Jab decided to use his gift again, like he had the day she Crossed. She remembered the pain, that hot flash in her temple, coming from nowhere. She and Pathik had just arrived at the temporary camp where Jab and Kinec, Pathik's trek companions, waited. Rachel had been shocked that she had actually Crossed, and was just beginning to realize that she might never be able to Cross back, that she might never see her mother again. But she hadn't yet thought to *fear* the Others, despite all the net books she had read about them, each filled with a more spectacular horror story than the last. When Pathik told her that Jab had caused the pain she felt, she realized that she knew nothing of them, not really. For the first time she had felt afraid of what the Others—even Pathik—might be capable of doing.

Rachel felt the faintest pang of that same fear when she saw Jab approach the fire. She knew that there had been a council meeting the night before to decide what punishment Jab would get for using his gift on her. It was forbidden for Others, at least the Others in Pathik's camp, to use their gifts without careful consideration.

"What's the verdict of the council?" Pathik didn't have to elaborate on his question; Jab knew what he meant.

"I'm to formally apologize." Jab kept his eyes on the campfire as he spoke. "To the camp and to her."

"That's all?" Pathik didn't sound pleased. "That's all they expect from you?"

Jab shrugged. "That and I'm to dredge all the common waste pots for the *entire* winter."

"Ha!" Pathik laughed. Emptying waste pots was drudgery. He was in charge of that chore for his household, so he knew it wasn't fun. But to have to do all the common pots, located throughout camp, for the entire winter? That would be a nightmare.

"Serves you right, Jab, and you know it."

Jab shrugged again. He leaned forward so he could see past Pathik, and waited until Rachel turned to look at him. "I do apologize," he said.

"Not good enough, Jab." Pathik's voice gained an edge.

Rachel knew that Pathik could tell whether Jab was sincere by using his gift; he could sense what others were feeling. *She* could tell without any gift at all that Jab didn't mean a word of his apology, but she didn't really care.

"It's fine," she said, turning away from Jab. She didn't want to prolong the interaction with him.

"Rachel." Pathik's voice was softer now. He waited for

her to look at him. When she did, he continued. "It's not fine. He hurt you." Pathik held her gaze for a moment, but then color infused his cheeks and he dropped his eyes. Rachel was glad he had looked down first; something in the look they exchanged had made her feel . . . *feelings*; feelings she didn't want to think about right now. She hoped Pathik wasn't aware of them; his gift might make that possible.

"A *formal* apology, Jab," said Pathik. "As the council decreed."

Jab groaned, but he stood up. He walked over and stood in front of Rachel, staring at her feet. She eyed him warily. He looked miserable.

"I am shamed by my actions." Jab hesitated. He heaved a huge sigh.

"I regret . . ." Pathik prompted.

"I *know,*" hissed Jab, rolling his eyes. "I regret the harm I have caused. I apologize to you, Rachel Quillen. Will you name reparations?"

"Reparations?" Rachel crinkled her brow at Pathik. "What does that mean?"

"To provide compensation, to make amends, to—"

"Oh, I know what it means. What does it *mean*, though?" Rachel shook her head at Pathik's grin. Sometimes he could be exasperating.

"It means what it sounds like. You can ask Jab to do something, or even to give you something of his, to try and make up for what he did." Pathik grinned even wider at the look on Jab's face.

Rachel didn't think any of it was funny. "Can't I just say 'apology accepted' and leave it at that?"

Pathik quickly grew serious. "That's what usually happens, although there is a traditional way to say it. I think actually naming reparations was something that was done long ago. At least I don't remember anybody naming reparations recent—"

"What's the traditional response?" Normally, Rachel would have been fascinated by the details of how society functioned Away. At least she would have when she was still safe on The Property, like she had been less than two weeks ago. Right now, all she wanted was to get Jab out of her sight.

"We say: 'I ask only that you remember this and do better,'" said Pathik.

Rachel looked up at Jab. She knew she should just say the phrase and have done with it, but he looked so wretched. She tilted her head up at him, watching him through narrowed eyes. After what he'd done to her, she wanted his misery to last just a little while longer.

"Pathik. Rachel." Nandy called their names quietly from a few yards away. "You're both to come."

Pathik looked to be sure Rachel was coming and hurried to Nandy. When she saw the look on Pathik's face, Nandy immediately reassured him.

"All is well—Malgam's not worse. In fact, he was the one who sent for you."

"I couldn't tell," said Pathik. He hadn't tried to scan

Nandy for emotion; as all the Others did, he avoided using his gift on people he knew, unless he was practicing and had permission. But even without trying, he had felt something from her; her emotions were big lately, because Malgam had been so close to dying. Without focusing on her, he hadn't been able to tell if it was joy or anguish.

"I imagine he wants to have a look at this one." Nandy nodded at Rachel and smiled.

Rachel smiled back. She liked Nandy, had liked her right away, late that first night in camp. Nandy was close to Rachel's mother's age, though she didn't look like Vivian at all. Her hair was cut short and jagged, and her pale gray eyes were more frankly appraising than Vivian's. There was something about her that reminded Rachel of Vivian though, some maternal, protective quality. That first night, Nandy had been the one who finally told the rest of the camp that Rachel *had* to get some sleep. She had shushed all their urgent questions with a wave of her hand, and dismissed them.

It also didn't hurt that Nandy's name didn't mean anything.

Jab's name referred to his gift. Pathik's name too. But as far as Rachel could tell, Nandy just meant . . . *Nandy*. Which meant that Nandy probably didn't have a gift. No special power. Nothing for Rachel to fear. So it was easier to trust her.

The Others named their children after the gifts they developed, if they developed any. Pathik had explained to Rachel that not all the Others developed gifts, so they kept their common names—the names they were given at birth. Nandy was a common name, and because she had never developed a gift, Nandy kept it as an adult. Even Indigo had never shown any signs of a special talent from what Rachel understood, and he had kept his common name, which was chosen because of the unusual color of his eyes.

Rachel thought most of the Others did develop something, even if it was nothing much. Kinec—the other boy who had been with Pathik and Jab when they made the trek to the Line—was named for his ability to move objects. He could make a fully loaded pack hop along the ground like a clumsy frog.

He had shown Rachel on the last night they spent together on their journey to Pathik's camp, just before they all wrapped up in the thermal blankets Ms. Moore had sent with them. The Others were taught not to show their gifts, but Pathik had said they could make an exception. And so, Kinec had placed his pack on the ground near the small campfire. He had stared at the pack intently, for so long that Rachel thought maybe nothing was going to happen. But then, the pack had lurched forward a few inches. Then it had actually leaped, not high, just half a foot off the ground, but it *left the ground*. It did that three times before Kinec grunted and collapsed.

"That's all I've got right now," he had said, beads of perspiration glittering on his brow.

Rachel was pretty sure Pathik had let Kinec show her his gift to make her feel better, to let her know that not all gifts were about causing physical pain. But when she remembered that pack, jerking forward like a clumsy bullfrog brought back from the dead, somehow she wasn't comforted.

"Now remember, he's still not strong." Nandy stopped at the door of the largest building in camp, a one-story brick structure that was still in pretty good repair. Rachel had imagined many former uses for that building in the last few days: a beauty salon, or a flower shop that might have sold orchids like the ones Ms. Moore grew—the ones she had been learning to grow too, before she Crossed. She had settled on a bakery, probably because she had been hungry most of the last two weeks and it was appealing to make mental lists of all the different kinds of desserts the shop might have offered.

There were a couple of other, smaller buildings near the bakery building, remnants of a town that must have stood there years ago. Before the Line was activated. They were constructed of some sort of gray blocks. She had slept in one of them since she had arrived in camp, in a cramped room with another girl around her age, who said as little as possible to her. There was still pavement visible in front of one of the buildings, a sidewalk from a lost time, crumbled and cracked. It reminded Rachel of one of the stranger sights she had seen on their trek from the Line to the camp.

They had been making their way through some dense underbrush, the boys hacking away at vines and bushes in order to clear a path. Jab had grumbled, and Pathik had said, "The road is coming up. It'll get easier for a while."

"Road?" Rachel saw nothing but brush and trees and wilderness everywhere she looked.

"There it is." Kinec pointed off to the left.

Rachel turned to look. She saw no road. What she did see was a corridor of strangely tamed landscape. There were some smaller saplings, and some bushes at intervals, but for a long stretch, as far as she could see, the wild forest was reduced to low scrub.

They headed for the easier terrain and once there, Rachel could see why it was so different from the rest of the forest. There were places—where a sapling had pushed up from the earth, or erosion had worn away enough top-soil—where she could see chunks of concrete. On one large chunk there was even a strip of faded, barely perceptible yellow paint.

They were walking on top of what had been, many years before, a highway.

NANDY RAPPED HER knuckles on the metal door. It was intact, if a bit rusted. On it were the two blue circles Rachel saw everywhere in camp; they were painted on all the doors, and she had seen them on tree trunks at the camp's perim-eter. When she'd asked Pathik about them he'd shrugged.

"They mark our camp." He had said no more.

There was no glass in the windows of the building; that must have shattered long ago. Someone had covered some of the smaller openings with wood. A piece of sheet metal covered the largest window—the one Rachel pictured filled with displays of pastries and cakes.

Nandy rapped again, and the door opened a crack, then wider. A man stood just inside. He had wavy black hair that reached his shoulders and he looked tired. Rachel was beginning to think that she would never see another person who *didn't* look tired.

"This her?" The man inspected Rachel. She stared back at him. She was growing weary of being evaluated by everyone she met in camp.

Nandy shot the man a look that Rachel couldn't decipher. "Let's go," she said.

Rachel patted her jacket pocket; the letters were there. She had had one each for Pathik, Malgam, and Indigo, from Ms. Moore. She had given them all to Pathik on the trek to camp, but he'd kept only his, saying that she should be the one to give Indigo and Malgam theirs. She hadn't known when the time would be right to give them out, so she had been carrying them around with her. She had already read the letter Ms. Moore had written for her, and the one her mom had written too. They were both brief; there hadn't been much time to waste before she Crossed. Ms. Moore's said to be careful, and to trust only Indigo, his family, and her own instincts. Her mom's said how much she loved Rachel, and told her to be strong. It also mentioned some maps that Vivian had slipped into Rachel's bag. Rachel had reread them both many times already.

Inside the building, the man who had opened the door

held a glass jar filled with some sort of oil, with a burning wick wired to the top. The flame cast a smoky yellow circle around the four of them, but the rest of the room was indistinct, cloaked in shadows. Pathik took Rachel's hand in his, to help guide her along. He had done this often on their trek to camp, but not once since they had arrived. Rachel had sort of missed it.

"Malgam's in a mood," said the man as he led them down a corridor off the main room.

"When has he ever *not* been in a mood?" Pathik sounded irritated.

"I'll take him moody and breathing over sweet and dead, anytime." Nandy's tone was light, but she shot a reproving look at Pathik.

The man knocked twice on the door at the end of the corridor. They could hear footsteps as someone walked toward the door.

"I'll leave you to it," said the man. He quickly disappeared back down the corridor.

Rachel was eager to see Indigo again. There were so many things she wanted to tell him: how much Ms. Moore had loved him, how much she thought Ms. Moore regretted not running Away with him all those years ago, how happy she had been when she discovered that he and her son were still alive. She wanted to ask him why he had stayed Away when Ms. Moore didn't meet him as they had planned, why he had never come back to see why she didn't. But most of all, she wanted to ask him about her father, Daniel. Pathik had refused to tell her anything. She had even asked the girl who shared her sleeping quarters, but she had just stared blankly at the digim of Daniel when Rachel showed it to her.

It was dark in the corridor without the wavy-haired man's light, and the way he had rushed off made her a little nervous. She wondered why he wanted to get away so quickly.

The footsteps they had heard approach the door stopped on the other side of it. Rachel could feel that someone was right there, separated from her and Pathik and Nandy by just inches, but there was no sound.

And then the doorknob started to turn.

CHAPTER 2

THE DOOR OPENED wide, spilling gold light into the dim corridor. Indigo stood there, smiling. He was a big man, strong despite his years. "I am so glad you could come." He looked at Rachel.

"Is . . . is Malgam better now, sir?"

"So much better! As you are about to see with your own eyes, child. Come in, come in all of you, Rachel, Pathik, Nan—" Indigo's eyes dropped to Rachel's hand, still clasped in Pathik's, and his eyebrows rose. Pathik was looking past Indigo toward the interior of the room and didn't notice at first. When he did notice, he dropped Rachel's hand as though he'd been burned, and pushed past her into the room. Rachel felt her cheeks flush. She ignored Nandy's smile and followed Pathik into the room.

The room they entered was large. More oil-filled jars lit the interior; the windows were covered with boards here too. There was a retrofitted fireplace in the corner—

someone had used stone to build up a hearth, and there was a hole directly above it in the ceiling, a crude outlet for smoke. Rachel wondered how they kept rain from falling into the room. There were four beds. One had a metal bed frame, ancient and dinged, but sturdy enough. The other three were fashioned from wood—*real* wood. Rachel was still surprised—even after three days of sitting in front of a wood fire—at how much real wood there was here. Some was old, from times when wood was still used in those ways, but some was from after the Line was activated. She could tell which were the newer pieces—they were roughly made, fashioned from the trunks of trees with what must be, from the looks of the cuts, crude tools. Only the metal bed was occupied. Malgam lay in it, his upper body propped up by pillows, his lower body covered with blankets. He was wearing a shirt made of the same coarse fabric Rachel had seen so much of in camp. Clothes, packs, bedding, tents, all were made of some version of the brownish, rough-woven cloth. She wondered who made it. Her own clothing, made of the various microfibers that were ubiquitous back home, often got looks here, and more than one of the Others had asked to touch her jacket.

Malgam was talking in a low voice to Pathik, who had seated himself on the edge of the bed. They both fell silent when Indigo led Rachel and Nandy closer.

"That the girl?" Malgam scowled in Rachel's general direction.

Indigo stood behind Rachel, so she couldn't see him,

but she felt his hands on her shoulders. She couldn't decide whether she felt comforted by them, or trapped.

"This," he said, in a tone that reminded her of the one her mother used when she was displeased, "is *the girl*. Her name is Rachel, as you already know, son. As you also already know, she saved your life." Indigo's fingers tapped lightly on Rachel's shoulders.

Malgam jutted his chin out and looked past Rachel to Indigo. He said nothing. Pathik widened his eyes at Rachel as though to say *This should be good*. She wished she could disappear.

"Malgam." Indigo spoke softly.

Malgam inhaled sharply, through his nose. He released the breath in a sigh, and shook his head. The corners of his mouth curled up a few centimeters.

"I know, Da. Manners, manners." He sighed again. "Rachel," he said, in a gentler voice, looking directly into her eyes, "I am pleased to meet you. If my son will kindly find you a chair, I hope you will visit for a bit. I hear we have much to talk about."

Pathik hopped off the bed and brought three battered metal chairs from where they were lined up against the far wall. He stationed one close to the head of Malgam's bed, and placed the other two at the foot. He gestured to Rachel to take a seat in the one closest to Malgam. Indigo and Nandy settled in the remaining two chairs, and Pathik stood behind Nandy.

Rachel kept her eyes on Malgam as she sat. There was

a pallor about him, and though she could see he had made some effort to tidy himself, his hair was mussed from bed rest and he smelled sour.

"First, I must give you thanks." He reached out toward her with both hands, and before she could stop herself Rachel jerked backward.

Malgam dropped his hands in his lap. He looked away from Rachel, at Indigo.

"See? Regs. They're all the same."

Rachel knew "Reg" stood for *regular*. It was what the Others called people like her—people from the other side of the Line.

Indigo rose from his seat and gripped the foot of the bed. He leaned toward Malgam, and the look on his face made Rachel press back even harder in her chair.

"How many Regs have you actually met, Malgam?" Indigo spoke quietly, but his tone was scornful. "This one"—he pointed at Rachel without looking at her—"has risked discovery and punishment, as have her friends and family. She has spent days traveling away from all she has ever known, without knowing whether she will ever be able to return home. She has done all that to bring medicine to a stranger—to *you*, Malgam." Indigo shook his head sadly. "You owe her more than thanks, my son. You owe her an apology."

Malgam began a retort, but Indigo held up his hand for silence.

"Daniel was a Reg. Do you hold *him* in contempt?"

"Daniel proved himself our friend many times over. He never flinched just because he was near one of us. He never judged us from the stories he heard, he—"

"Yet you judge Rachel for a reflex you can hardly begrudge her. You know what Jab did to her. Why should she trust any of us, after that? Would you be so—"

"What do you mean '*was* a Reg'?" Rachel's voice was quiet, but there was a quality to it—an urgency—that made the others in the room listen. "Is he alive or dead?"

There was silence. Rachel felt all eyes on her. She met each person's gaze, one by one, but none said anything to her. Finally she looked at back at Malgam.

"I'm glad that you're better. I didn't mean to offend you. I think I'm just . . . I'm just tired, I guess." Rachel felt tears in her eyes and fought them back. "I've been here three days and I haven't seen him, and nobody will talk to me about him, but you *know* him, you *know* who he is. Pathik knew his name." She looked at Pathik, and saw sadness in his eyes. It tipped the balance she had been struggling to maintain, and tears spilled onto her cheeks. "He's my father. I just want to know if he is alive."

Malgam looked stricken. He leaned forward in the bed, and reached his hands out once more, smiling a gentle question to her. Rachel hesitated only a moment before placing her hands in his.

"Forgive me, Rachel." Malgam bowed his head. When he looked up again he squeezed her hands gently and nodded.

"We will talk of Daniel. But first, I do need to thank you

for saving my life. By our traditions it is important. And so I tender my thanks to you, Rachel." He raised their joined hands up. "If ever I can help you, know that I will. For what you have done, you will always be welcome to my shelter, my fire, my water, my food." He squeezed her hands once more and smiled at her. "Not so bad, was it?"

She smiled back, despite her tears. "Not so bad."

Malgam released her hands. "Now. When was the last time you saw Daniel?"

"I was little." Rachel wiped her eyes dry. "I don't really know if I remember him, or if I just remember what my mother has told me about him. He got a Call to Serve from the government, and they sent my mother a death notice only a short time after he reported for duty."

"Call to Serve?" Malgam looked at Indigo.

Indigo nodded. "Daniel said it was one of the ways the government gets rid of people they suspect of being rebels. They summon them, as if they need them in some war effort. Then they get rid of them and claim they were killed in action. It's what happened to him."

"You spoke with him?" Rachel searched Indigo's face. "When? Where is he?"

Indigo's eyes looked as sad as Pathik's had moments before. Rachel looked from him to each of the others in the room, and they all wore the same expression.

"He's dead, isn't he?"

"We don't know that, Rachel." Nandy was the one who spoke. "He hasn't come to camp in months, and that isn't normal, even for Daniel. He's always kept to himself, but he's also always checked in, to see if all was well, or to trade for supplies. We didn't know what to think for a long time, but now we have reason to suspect that the Roberts may have him."

"Who?" It seemed to Rachel that things had sped up; it was hard to keep up with what Nandy was saying through the thoughts that were racing through her mind. Daniel *had* been here. Her father. Alive. A few days' walk from The Property this whole time.

"—just always called them that since then." Nandy frowned. "Are you all right, Rachel?"

"Yes." Rachel forced herself to focus on Nandy. "So, who is this Robert? What would he want with my father?"

"Not Robert," said Nandy. "*Roberts*. Plural. It's another group. In the beginning it's said they were led by a man named Robert, and they've been called the Roberts since then. Their camp is less than a day away from here, but they keep their distance." Nandy looked worried. "They're no good."

"And you think they have my father? Why?"

Indigo spoke. "We think they may be planning to use him as a bargaining tool. Several days before Pathik came to you, Rachel, one of the Roberts was discovered near camp. He was injured—someone from his own camp had stabbed him, because he had decided to leave. They don't let people leave."

"Had he seen my father? Can I talk to him?"

"He died shortly after we brought him here. But before he died, he told us that the Roberts had a stranger in a cage. He said they were going to trade him to the government. We'd planned a council meeting to put together a rescue attempt, but then Malgam worsened to the point where we thought he would die and we had to focus on that." Indigo considered Rachel for a moment. "How much," he asked, "do you know about your father, Rachel?"

"I know he was a collaborator."

"A collaborator." Indigo frowned. "He called it that too. That word sounds so . . . bad."

"Most people think they *are* bad."

"Daniel wasn't . . . *isn't* bad." Indigo looked pained.

Rachel shrugged. "I wouldn't know," she said.

"What do you mean?"

"I mean I wouldn't *know*," said Rachel. "I wouldn't know if he was good, or bad, or somewhere in between. I haven't seen him since I was three years old. Even though he has apparently been alive and well just a few days' travel away, this whole time." Rachel flung her words at Indigo like stones.

Malgam pushed his blankets back as though he might rise. "Do you think a parent would leave his child, ever? *Ever*, if he knew that child was alive and needing him? No *good* parent would."

Nandy silenced Malgam with a glare and stepped closer to Rachel. "Oh, Rachel." She put a hand on Rachel's shoulder and squeezed. "He thought you were dead. You *and* your mother—he thought they had killed you both." Nandy's eyes glittered. "It almost killed *him*."

"Why would he think we were dead?" Rachel wasn't moved. "Doesn't sound like he bothered to check."

"He did bother." Malgam ignored Nandy's renewed glare. "Unlike some."

"Enough." Indigo shook his head at Malgam. He sat back down in his chair. "Daniel did try to find you, Rachel. He had a contact on the other side, and we were able to get word to him. But you and your mother were gone." He looked at Rachel intently. "I know he would have found a way to get back to you if he had thought for one minute you were alive. He would have stopped at nothing. Just as we must stop at nothing now. If your father is being held by the Roberts, we have to get him out of there. They *will* kill him eventually, or worse."

"We left . . . we left the city as soon as my mother knew he was dead. We ran. Mom found a job with Ms. Moore on The Property." Rachel thought, a realization dawning. "Maybe whoever he checked with thought we really *were* dead."

Indigo cleared his throat. "How . . . how is Elizabeth?"

Rachel noticed all the others in the room fell silent. Malgam had his eyes lowered, but Pathik and Nandy were both watching Indigo.

"She's . . . fine." Rachel thought about how Ms. Moore had waved, and kept waving, as Rachel got farther and farther away after she Crossed. How finally she couldn't see Ms. Moore—or her mom—anymore.

"Good." Indigo nodded. "That's good." He seemed to realize he was still nodding, and stopped. "Well."

"She wrote to you, to each of you." Rachel brought out the letters she had tucked in her jacket. Gravely she handed each to its recipient; the envelopes were labeled in Ms. Moore's neat hand.

"This is from Elizabeth?" Indigo ran a finger over his name on the envelope.

"If we're going after Daniel, we need to do it quickly." Malgam watched Indigo with a tenderness Rachel hadn't thought he possessed. He seemed hesitant to change the subject.

"We'll need today to prepare and to have a council meeting." Nandy looked like she was making lists in her head. "I think Rachel should move out of the visitors' quarters and in with us."

"That girl is a visitor? From where?" Rachel had wondered why the girl who shared the room she slept in wasn't with a family. She and Rachel seemed to be the only people who didn't live with a family group.

"She showed up not long after the Roberts man who died. We put her there because we aren't sure what to make of her." Nandy saw Rachel's confusion. "We think she came from the Roberts. There aren't many lone survivors out there, if any, so she must have. We don't know if we can trust her."

"So the people you don't trust sleep in that room?" Rachel was half teasing.

"Yes." Nandy wasn't teasing at all. "But I think we all feel like we can trust you now. You've not tried anything strange, and you have helped as much as you can in camp. I heard you gathered fire twigs yesterday. And I'm told you don't complain, at least not much." Nandy grinned at Pathik.

"You rest as much as you can," Indigo said to Malgam. He pointed at Nandy and Pathik. "You two get Rachel settled. I am going to call a council for tonight. I think we will leave in the morning, and we'll want to have a plan."

They went their separate ways: Nandy to help Rachel fetch her things to their rooms, which were in one of the hand-built huts, and Pathik to gather firewood for the family hearth. Indigo went to call the council together. Malgam stayed where he was, and tried, as much as he could, not to dwell on the sadness he'd seen in his father's eyes at the mention of his mother. He looked at the envelope in his hands, at his name, written in his mother's slanted cursive—a script he'd never seen before. It was fashioned from a fine paper, thin as leaves, unlike anything he had seen, save for the pages of the few books they had in camp, or the notebook filled with information the first survivors thought they might need. He fingered the corner of the seal. But then he shook his head and placed the envelope on the table next to his bed. He didn't want to know what she had to say, at least not now.

CHAPTER 3

ELIZABETH DABBED AT the corners of her mouth with her napkin—a fine linen napkin from a different era.

"That was, as usual, delicious, Vivian."

Rachel's mother smiled from across the breakfast table. The two women had taken to eating together for most meals, and had developed, during the last weeks, an almost easy familiarity. It was a drastic change from how things had been for the last twelve years on The Property, when the lines between employee and employer were formally drawn and strictly observed. Rachel's Crossing had altered all of that.

"I'm glad you liked it. I'm hoping to pick up some more of that honey in town today." Vivian's smile didn't overcome her wan complexion, or the deep lines around her mouth and eyes. She looked ten years older than she had a month before. She rose and began to clear the dishes. Elizabeth stood as well, and reached for a glass.

"You go start in the greenhouse," said Vivian. "You'll only slow me down in here. I'll be out to help with the trays soon."

"All right, come when you can, but no hurry. Jonathan will be out there by now."

JONATHAN, MS. MOORE'S hired hand, *was* in the greenhouse, moving trays of orchid starts to the bench where Elizabeth and Vivian would pot them. He paused to watch Elizabeth approach. When she got inside the door he spoke.

"Is Ms. Quillen any better today?"

"Maybe a bit less exhausted looking. But she really has me worried." Elizabeth shook her head. "Any word on Peter?"

"Nothing new," said Jonathan. "I drove out past his place in town."

"You what?"

"I was careful. Never slowed down a bit, just one more vehicle on the road." He set the last of the trays on the bench.

"And?"

"Nothing. No sign of life there, no vehicle, shut up tight as a drum." Jonathan tilted his ever-present hat back off his forehead and scratched an eyebrow with gnarled fingers. "I'd say he's gone. Whether the EOs took him or whether he went on his own is hard to tell."

Elizabeth didn't reply. She thought it might be best if

Enforcement Officers *had* taken Peter. She was afraid he had planned, that night he came to The Property, to turn Vivian in to the government. He must have thought he could get the authorities to release his wife and daughter in trade. Even Vivian, who had initially trusted him enough to ask him for help, was beginning to believe he might have betrayed her now.

Every night since Rachel had Crossed with Pathik, Elizabeth and Vivian had dissected that evening, looking at it from one vantage point and then another. They had talked it over and over, until all their words on the subject were smooth, well-worn stones. Vivian often tried to defend Peter's treachery, asking Elizabeth how she would behave if her loved ones were at risk. Elizabeth maintained that even though his wife and daughter had been Identified and hauled away, he had no reason to betray old friends. If Peter hadn't brought the EOs with him that night, Rachel would still be safe, on this side of the Line. Elizabeth was just grateful that the EOs had seemed to believe their story about Rachel being a runaway easily enough.

Elizabeth potted orchids as she thought, her hands automatically performing the task she had done so many times. She wondered where Rachel and Pathik were now. She hoped they had made it to . . . wherever Indigo and Malgam were. She hoped the medicine had arrived in time to save Malgam's life.

Malgam. Her son. The son she had not seen since he was an infant, because of her own cowardliness. And Indigo. She wondered if he thought of her, if he tried to imagine what her life was like now.

"What about these?" Jonathan's hands holding one of the orchid starts she had just potted, swam into focus before her.

"Those are the last crosses Rachel did before . . ."

"I know," said Jonathan. "Should I put them in with the other starts?"

"No. No, I think we'll keep those separate. I don't want to sell those." Elizabeth was surprised to feel tears pricking her eyes. "Put them in the west section on the middle shelves, will you, Jonathan? And then could you check the hoses over there—I think that one you repaired is still leaking." She wiped her hands on a towel and started on the next tray of plants.

Jonathan made sure to look away, so Elizabeth wouldn't see his grin. She had sounded almost like her old, imperious self just then, and the sound made him feel good. He'd long ago given up hope that she could ever love him, yet he still loved her. Not as he had when they were both young, of course. His love had changed over the years to the sort that expected nothing, and generally got it. Still, it was there. He hoped she knew it in some way, and took some small comfort from it, even if he wasn't the one she had wanted.

He placed the tray of Rachel's starts on the middle shelf and eyed the connector he had replaced on one of the old hoses. Sometimes he wondered how they kept this operation going, with everything wearing out the way it was, and no shortage of shortages on the parts required to fix things.

He wouldn't be surprised when the day came that he or Ms. Quillen drove into Bensen for supplies and there just plain weren't any. The world wasn't the same as it once had been.

His eye caught a movement through the greenhouse glass, out past the Line. He squinted. Felt that old fear crawling up his spine, even though he knew he shouldn't be afraid. The Others weren't the monsters he'd been raised to believe they were, at least not according to Elizabeth. She should know. She had a child with one of them.

More movement, and a deer materialized in the meadow. Jonathan released the breath he had been holding, and snorted at his own silliness. Still, he knew plenty in the county who wouldn't call it foolish. Plenty believed every hyped-up story they heard about the Others. As Elizabeth had pointed out, the Others were a good diversion when the latest shipment of food didn't arrive or somebody's son got Identified for a random tax, or because they couldn't find Gainful Employment. As she would say, *Give people something simple to hate and fear, and they will hate and fear with a passion.* Jonathan nodded to himself.

"It keeps 'em busy." He snorted again, and started unscrewing the hose coupling.

VIVIAN FINISHED PUTTING the dishes away and went to the closet in the hall to get her jacket and scarf. She shrugged the jacket on and wrapped the scarf snugly around her neck. It was getting chilly out.

It was getting chilly out.

Instantly, from some never-ending source, tears came. Rachel was out there. Was she warm enough? Had they made it to that camp? Was there shelter? Were the people there treating her well? The questions kept coming. At breakfast: Did Rachel have enough to eat? At night: Was she sleeping now? And on and on, in an endless refrain. The biggest question, the worst question, was one that never stopped repeating itself in the back of her mind. While she did the housekeeping chores, while she helped in the greenhouse, while she tried to fall asleep at night.

"Will I ever see her again?" Vivian whispered it to herself, almost humming. It had become a song of sorts, a song she hated. She wiped her eyes with the end of the scarf and turned to go.

And heard the soft beep of the streamer.

Ms. Moore never got vocalls or comms. Her contact information wasn't listed on the public roster—Vivian had no idea whom she paid off to accomplish that, or how much she paid them—and she didn't seem to have any friends. So that streamer beep almost never happened. It couldn't mean good news.

Vivian edged toward the parlor, where the streamer was. Sure enough, the blue light glowed and dimmed in sequence, signaling a message. Vivian touched the screen. Its opacity cleared and an incoming vocall log line appeared.

"It's from Peter." Vivian drew her hand back as though a snake had appeared on the screen. She stared at the log line, as if it might disappear. Then she pulled out the stool in front of the streamer and sat down. After another moment, she touched the screen again, and the comm opened. It was brief.

> I'm Crossing. If I find Rachel I will try to bring her back to you. I need what she has.
> I never wanted to hurt you. I didn't call them— they must have been watching.

Vivian sat very still. She focused on breathing very slowly, deep breaths through her nose that she exhaled through pursed lips. She was still sitting there when Elizabeth found her, thirty minutes later.

"HE MUST PLAN to use his key, then." Elizabeth and Jonathan sat in the two stiff chairs flanking the fireplace in the parlor. Vivian was now on the couch, where she refused to recline despite Elizabeth's encouragement.

"Yes." Vivian nodded and took a sip of the kalitea Elizabeth had made. Her hands were shaking, so she set the cup on the table.

"So you think he really had a key?" Jonathan held the delicate china cup Elizabeth had given him in both hands, as though he held the last egg of some endangered species of bird.

"I know he had at least one." Vivian shivered, though

the house was warm. "You know, it could be that he *didn't* call the EOs that night. He did seem surprised when they showed up."

"I figured that for an act, but I guess it could have been real." Jonathan squinted at his kalitea. "If he had called them, why wouldn't he have just turned you in when they got here?" He looked up at Vivian and Elizabeth. "Really, for all that, why would he have come here at all? Couldn't he have just made a call?"

Elizabeth nodded. "It's true. He could have just called them if he was planning on turning you in."

"I don't know anymore." Vivian left her cup where she had set it. "I've thought and thought and I don't know *what* I would have done if it had been Daniel and Rachel dragged off by the EOs. I don't know . . . maybe *I* would betray a friend." She shook her head slowly. "I don't think so, though. I hope Peter didn't either."

"Well, there's nothing we can do." Elizabeth frowned. "All we can do is hope he does bring her back."

Vivian smiled at that. "Yes," she said. "Maybe he will. Maybe he really will bring her back." She didn't notice the look that passed between Elizabeth and Jonathan.

"Thing is, the EOs are probably looking for him now. If he shows up anywhere on this side of the Line again, they're sure to be scanning for him, so—" Jonathan stopped talking when he saw the look on Elizabeth's face.

"Who knows what will happen." Elizabeth shook her head at Jonathan. It was too much for Vivian to think about now. She was barely holding on as it was. "We can only wait, for now. Wait and hope."

Vivian nodded. She had been wondering, the past few weeks, about hope. She had a feeling—a feeling that she didn't want to have—that hope might actually be a terrible, terrible thing.

CHAPTER 4

RACHEL WAS GLAD the girl she had been sharing the room with wasn't there when she and Nandy went to get her things. She wouldn't have known what to say to her if she had been. *Hi, I'm moving out of this room, because they trust me now. Hope they trust you soon.* She wondered if they really did trust her now. Or if she trusted them.

Nandy grabbed the bigger of Rachel's bags, the duffel bag that Ms. Moore had packed. Rachel hadn't had time to go through all of the things in it. She took the bag her mom had packed.

"Anything else?" Nandy waited at the door.

"Nothing."

"Oh." Nandy dropped the duffel. "Let's get the blanket and the pillow. Not that many extras around here." She stripped the cot quickly and handed the bedding to Rachel, then lifted the duffel bag again.

"This thing is heavy." Suddenly she grew excited. "Does it have books in it?"

"No." Rachel thought it was an odd question. "Why?"

"Pathik said he thought you had ... everything ... where you came from. I just thought you might have books."

"Do you have books here?" Rachel felt, somehow, as if a great deal depended upon Nandy's answer to that question.

Nandy nodded. "A few. Not as many as I would like. I think there were *many* books, before." Nandy studied her. "*Are* there many where you came from? Pathik said there must be."

"Millions of net books. And there are old-fashioned ones at the library."

Nandy kept looking at Rachel, conflicting emotions battling on her face. "We," she said in a brittle tone, "have twenty-three. Twenty-three books. Though I think we are especially lucky, because one of them is a dictionary." She lowered her eyes and did not look at Rachel for several moments. When she raised them again she seemed more herself, more the sunny Nandy Rachel had come to expect during her short time at camp. "Let's get to home."

Home turned out to be one of the largest of the huts that dotted the camp. As they got closer Rachel could see it had been constructed from rocks, many years before, judging from the lichen and moss growing on it. Some sort of mortar blocked the cracks and crevices, but the stones were fit together so expertly that it looked like they would hold without any help. The door, which was emblazoned with the obligatory blue circles that every door in the camp seemed to have, was fashioned from a piece of sheet metal that didn't fit the wooden door frame well. There was cloth bundled into the gap. Nandy took hold of the edge of the cloth before she opened the door so it wouldn't fall to the ground. She gestured to Rachel to enter. When they were both through she pulled the door shut after them and stuffed the cloth back into the gap.

"We keep meaning to get a better door." She sounded apologetic.

Rachel followed Nandy into a large room. It took her a moment to adjust to the change in light.

"You can put your bags here for now." Nandy put Ms. Moore's duffel bag on the floor near the door and walked toward what looked like a hearth. Rachel dropped her bag next to Ms. Moore's and followed. She could see two doorways off the main room that must be sleeping areas. When Nandy lit an oil jar she saw a large table surrounded by stools.

Rachel froze in place. In the middle of the table lay a . . . creature. It was about the size of a lynx. Rachel had studied lynx back at The Property, as part of a home schooling lesson Vivian prepared about extinct animals; lynx in particular had captivated her because of their beauty, but also because of something—some fine awareness—in their faces.

The creature on the table looked a lot like a lynx in some ways. It had large ears, and emerald, slanted eyes set in a pointed face. It possessed a sinewy grace evident even in repose. It had that same fine awareness Rachel had admired in lynx. But instead of fur, this creature was covered in short, dense wool. The wool was curly, and striped like a domestic tabby cat. Rachel knew that it must be one of the peculiar creatures described in her net books about Away.

"A . . . sheep-cat," she whispered.

"What?" Nandy shrugged off her coat.

Rachel pointed at the creature. "I think . . . Is that a sheep-cat?"

"What's a sheep-cat?" Nandy walked over to the table and sat down. She stroked the long, muscled back of the animal. "How was your day, Nipper?" The creature made no reply; it stared at Rachel, inscrutable.

Rachel hesitated. "I've read about those, I think. In the books they called them sheep-cats. But they were described as much larger, and vicious too."

"Nipper's pretty big as Woollies go. Most are a bit smaller. But your books are right about the vicious part. If I managed to get close enough to touch a wild Woolly I would lose my hand. Not that you aren't wild, right, Nipper?" Nandy smiled and dug her fingers into the thick fleece behind the Woolly's ear. "He needed some help once, when he was a baby. I gave it. And we've been friends since." Nipper growled softly, still staring at Rachel.

"Have a seat. We have a lot to talk about." Nandy laughed when Rachel stayed where she was. "He's just saying hello. He won't hurt you, will you, Nipper?"

The Woolly turned his head and gazed at Nandy. He growled again, and tilted his head so her fingers found a new place to scratch.

Rachel edged toward the chair closest to her and slowly sat down. Nipper watched. When she was finally settled he lifted the left side of his lip in a sneer, revealing one long fang.

"So sheep-cats are real." Rachel thought about the fantastic stories she had loved to read about Away and wondered what other creatures described in them might turn out to actually exist.

"Have you started bleeding yet, Rachel?" Nandy's tone was all business now.

"Do you mean . . . menstruating?" Rachel kept her eyes on Nipper.

"Yes. If you have, we'll need to bring extra provisions on the trek. I doubt you had time to pack anything."

"I had the implant when I was born. Didn't . . . Oh, of course you didn't." Rachel felt the strange sense of disorientation that had been hitting her since she Crossed the Line. Every time she saw the battered pots and pans or flipped the useless light switch on the wall in her sleeping room, she realized all over again that she was *Away*, that the devastation from long-ago bombs and betrayal was real. These people had no modern conveniences. Any food they ate, they killed or grew; any clothing they wore, they made, from cloth they wove. They drank water they hauled from the stream, not water dispensed from condensation units. If someone grew ill, they could easily die. It was like nothing Rachel had ever experienced.

"I won't start menstruating until I get my repro clearance

and permission to have my implant removed. So no worries there."

"Repro clearance?"

"Permission to have a child." Nipper stretched one front leg out toward Rachel and showed off six bladed toes. Rachel stared at the claws, fascinated; they appeared to be serrated along their edges.

"Well." Nandy's face looked the way it had when they were talking about books. "We don't need permission here. Just luck."

"Is Pathik your only child?" Rachel wasn't certain why Nandy looked so angry.

"I love him like he is, but Pathik's not mine. His mother died giving birth to his younger brother."

"He has a brother?"

"He didn't live either." Nandy's eyes glittered at Rachel from across the table. Nipper growled again, low and long. "The woman who was the healer then couldn't help them. Even Saidon—she's our healer now—couldn't have helped them. She's got a great gift, but it's limited. If someone is truly dying, she can't heal them."

"Do . . . do you have any children?"

"Do you see any?" Nandy's voice was hard.

"I'm sorry."

Nandy shook her head, swiping at her eyes with one hand, calming Nipper with the other.

"It's not your fault, is it, Rachel? So it does me no good to be mad at you."

The door to the hut crashed open, and Pathik burst into the room with a stack of kindling.

"The wadding, Pathik! How many times do I have to remind you, hold on to the wadding so it doesn't fall. Or next time you do all the washing."

"Sorry, Nan." Pathik blinked at Nandy's tone. "I think it only got a little dusty." Pathik made a production of brushing the cloth off. "Time to go—they're all waiting. I told them they could meet Rachel today."

"Who? Who can meet me?"

"The children." Nandy rose and gave Nipper one more caress. "Time to go put that dictionary to use." She paused by Rachel, and put a hand on her shoulder. "Sorry. None of it is anybody's fault, at least nobody in this room." She smiled, though it was a weak version of her usual smile. "Let's go."

Rachel watched her walk out the door, Nipper fast on her heels. She looked at Pathik.

"Did I walk in on something? She's not usually snappish."

Rachel shook her head. "Nothing much." She looked at Pathik, taking in his tired eyes and his face, the face she had decided was handsome, even if its owner was often irritating. "I'm sorry about your mother, Pathik. And . . . and your brother."

"Why are *you* sorry? Has nothing to do with you." Pathik refused to meet her eyes.

"Because . . . because they died." Rachel brushed past him and headed for the door.

"Rachel." His quiet voice stopped her. She turned back to face him.

"Thanks." He looked at her intently. "For being sorry, I mean." He reached over and touched the collar of her jacket, just below her earlobe. "Are you going to be warm enough in this? The schoolroom doesn't have a fireplace."

"Schoolroom?" Rachel felt oddly warm, and somehow she couldn't drag her gaze from his.

Pathik grinned. He let his fingers slide off of her collar. "Nandy's our teacher. We're going to help her today."

CHAPTER 5

THE SCHOOLROOM TURNED out to be in the second of the smaller buildings. Like the building Rachel had been sleeping in, this one was made of some sort of gray block, and was utilitarian in its architecture. It did not have a door on the main entrance, which opened onto a single large room. As Pathik had said, there was no fireplace here. An aisle led up the center of the room, and on either side of it were rows of wooden benches. Rachel could see the marks left from a cutting tool, where someone planed the logs long ago. The rough cuts on the top sides of the logs were smoothed from years of use. Nipper was lounging on the bench closest to the door.

Nandy was already at the front of the room. She took three flat metal trays down from a shelf and put one on each of three small, low tables centered in the aisle between the rows of benches. Pathik motioned to Rachel to follow him to the front, where he took a large plastic bucket down from the shelf. He handed Rachel a bundle of pointed sticks.

"Three per tray," he said, and started down the aisle. At each tray, he tilted the bucket and dumped a mound of sand in. Nandy came along behind him and smoothed the sand flat with the edge of a flat scrap of wood. Then she fetched a metal bowl and poured a quantity of water from it into each tray. Rachel stood at the top of the aisle, uncertain exactly what to do.

"Here, Rachel." Nandy gestured for her to come. She took three of the sticks from the bundle and laid them next to the first tray. "Do the same with those." Nandy pointed to the two trays farther down the aisle. "Check the points to be sure they're sharp."

Rachel did as she was told. She didn't know why she was doing it, but at least it took her mind off of the upcoming rescue attempt. She'd been fighting thoughts about it all morning. What if they failed? What if they couldn't find her father, or worse, found him dead? She was glad for the distraction the task at hand offered.

Three little boys spilled through the door, laughing about something. They were followed by two girls. Soon there was a small crowd of children, milling and laughing and sometimes shouting at the back of the room.

"School time." Nandy's voice was low, but all of the children heard it immediately and turned to where she stood in the front of the room. When they saw Rachel they all fell silent for a moment, and then began buzzing loudly with speculation. Nandy grinned at Rachel. "They are quite excited to meet you." She turned back to the children.

"Seats, please." The buzzing faded and the children scrambled to find places on the benches. All eyes darted between Rachel and Nandy. Rachel took a rough count and figured the number at about twenty-five. The age range seemed to be from around six to twelve, and they looked well-fed and healthy as far as she could tell. She had seen children in the camp during the few days she had been present, but always at some distance.

Pathik had joined Rachel at the front of the room. He put a hand in front of his mouth and leaned toward her. "They've been begging Nandy since the day you arrived," he whispered. "They all want to see if you have fangs, or glow in the dark."

"We have a guest today." Nandy addressed the room. "I think you all know that we have a special visitor in camp, who helped Pathik get the medicine that Malgam needed to get well."

"She's a Reg."

Rachel didn't see who said it, but it wasn't said in a friendly tone.

"Bender." Nandy sounded disappointed. "Come to the front of the room, please."

A boy of about eleven stood. He stayed where he was, though, his head hung low.

"Bender. It's all right."

The boy kept his head down, but he shuffled his way forward until he was standing in front of Nandy.

"Bender, I want you to properly greet Rachel."

The boy raised his eyes and squinted at Nandy through dark lashes. He risked a sidelong glance at Rachel. "She's a Reg." He spoke so low Rachel could barely make out the words.

"We've talked about this before, Bender. Remember our history lesson last week? Do you remember what we learned about the people over there?"

Bender looked skeptical. "Some of them are good."

"That's right, Bender." Nandy sounded as pleased as if the child had solved some complex mathematical problem. "Some Regs are good. Remember how we learned about the collaborators? How they want to make things fair for everyone? Collaborators are Regs, and they're good. So it isn't if you're a Reg or not that makes you good or bad, right, Bender?"

Bender had raised his head while Nandy spoke. He peered at her face, and then at Rachel. "Right."

"What is it, Bender, that makes a person good or bad? Do you remember?"

Bender nodded. "It's what they *do*."

Nandy nodded back to him. "And what, to your knowledge, has Rachel done? Has she done anything bad?"

Bender squinted at Rachel. He bit his lower lip. He frowned at her, and squinted some more.

Rachel looked back at him. She smiled, tentatively. She shrugged her shoulders.

"Nothing bad I know of." Bender squinted at Nandy.

"And she did do good to help Pathik. So I guess, so far, she's good."

"So?" Nandy crossed her arms and waited.

Bender bit his lip again. He stepped sideways until he was in front of Rachel. He squinted up at her. "You, Rachel . . ." Bender faltered, looked at Nandy.

"Are welcome . . ." said Nandy.

Bender continued in a rush. ". . . are welcome to our shelter, our fire, our water, our food." He extended his hands to Rachel.

Pathik took Rachel's hands in his and placed them atop Bender's. "I thank you," he prompted in a whisper.

"I thank you." Rachel smiled at Bender.

Bender squinted at Rachel a moment longer. When he was satisfied with whatever he saw, he looked at Nandy, who nodded.

"Good job, Bender. Back to your seat." She addressed the rest of the children.

"Why does he keep wrinkling up his face like that?" Rachel whispered behind her hand to Pathik.

"Bender?" Pathik waited until Rachel nodded. "He's got some trouble with his eyes—he can't see well if things are farther than a few feet away from him."

"Oh," said Rachel. She knew some children were born with less than perfect sight, but it was always corrected immediately with lasers. Not so here. She couldn't imagine what it must be like to be unable to do something as basic as seeing.

Nandy clapped her hands twice, to get the attention of the class. "Time for spelling. Who can spell the word *agitate*?"

A girl stood and made her way to the tray at the end of her aisle. She took one of the sticks Rachel had placed in the tray and drew in the sand. Nandy came and looked at what the girl drew. "That's correct, Rose. A-G-I-T-A-T-E. And can you tell me the definition?" Nandy smoothed the damp sand in the tray with her wood scrap.

"To shake." Rose watched Nandy for approval, which she got in the form of Nandy's smile.

"And also?" Nandy waited while Rose thought.

"To make you mad." Rose turned to Bender. "You *agitate* me, Bender!" She giggled at him, and Bender laughed back. Soon the whole class was giggling.

"Brothers can tend to do that, Rose." Nandy stood with her hands on her hips, shaking her head at the class antics. She gave them a minute to get the energy out of their systems and then she raised her eyebrows and tilted her head in an exaggerated way. Once again, the class settled.

There were more words to spell, and as the lesson went on the children snuck fewer glances at Rachel and paid more attention to Nandy.

"She certainly has a way with them." Rachel spoke softly to Pathik, so she wouldn't be a distraction.

"That's Nandy's gift," said Pathik.

"You mean she's controlling them somehow?" Rachel was disturbed by the thought.

Pathik smiled and shook his head at her. "It's her *plain gift*. That's what we call it when someone just has a way—not something extra, like Jab, or me—but just a way with something. Nandy has a plain gift when it comes to the young ones."

"Why don't the ones with plain gifts get named for them?"

Pathik shrugged. "It usually takes longer for those kinds of gifts to surface. And sometimes people have more than one. With the other kind, you never get more than one."

Rachel considered that. She stole a glance at Pathik.

"You had a brother," she whispered. Pathik watched her, waiting to see what else she was going to say.

"And Rose." Rachel nodded toward the little girl. "Bender is *her* brother." She waited expectantly.

Pathik gave her a quizzical look. "Yes?"

"Rose and Bender are *siblings*."

Pathik just looked baffled.

"*A single child saves all children—one child limit, one child limit.*" Rachel uttered the slogan in a singsong tune, the way she had heard it all her life. "That's the law. One child. Nobody has siblings."

"Nobody?" Pathik sounded amazed. "We don't have many here, but when we do it's considered a great thing."

Rachel thought. "Well, Poolers can have more than one child, at least in some cases."

"What are Poolers?"

"Sort of . . . workers. You get put in Labor Pools if you

can't find Gainful Employment, or if you get Identified for something. Some people never get out. Some Poolers come from families who have been in the Pools for generations."

Rachel and Pathik both fell silent, thinking about how different their lives were.

The spelling lesson ended, and Nandy strode to the front of the room again. "Today," she said, "Usage is canceled. Indigo has called a council, so we'll need the room for that. Tomorrow, Indigo will be gone on trek, so Usage will be led by Saidon. For now, school is out and you are free to go!"

The children erupted in one joyous explosion and streamed out the door. Nandy laughed as she watched them go. She turned to Rachel and Pathik.

"Could you two tidy up? I'd better go make sure they all get where they should go."

Pathik nodded, and Nandy left, Nipper padding along behind.

"What's Usage?" Rachel retrieved the pointed sticks from the trays and bundled them back up. Pathik scooped the damp sand into one tray and stacked the other two on the shelf where they belonged. He set the third in the corner so the sand could dry.

When he was done he sat on the first bench and tilted his head toward the space next to him. "Might as well sit."

Rachel did, careful to leave enough space between them that they wouldn't accidentally touch. She could still feel her cheeks flood with warmth when she thought about him touching her collar back at the hut.

"Usage is what we call the lessons we have for learning about our gifts. About how to get better at them, and about the proper way to use them."

"Do you go to Usage?"

"Anyone who has a gift does, until Indigo grants us passage." Pathik was going to continue, but a boy poked his head in the doorway and cleared his throat.

"Council's coming. This room should be clear."

"We're invited to council today, Fisher."

Pathik's tone made Rachel turn and take a closer look at the boy. He looked slightly older than she and Pathik. He was tall, with wavy blond hair. From where she sat she couldn't see the color of his eyes, but she could tell he was appraising her with a certain interest. He entered the room, and walked up the aisle to stop in front of them.

"So this is Rachel, I take it. A very brave woman, from what I hear." He grinned at Pathik and then extended his hands to Rachel. "You, Rachel, are welcome to our shelter, our fire, our water, our food."

His eyes, upon closer inspection, were brown, and at the moment sparkling with humor. Rachel was noticing flecks of gold in them, tiny little flecks placed just so, when she realized that Fisher still stood with his hands extended to her. Both he and Pathik were staring at her, one with an irritated look and the other with a rather open appraisal. She jumped to her feet and placed her hands on top of Fisher's.

"I thank you," she said gravely.

"Since Pathik doesn't seem eager to do the honors, let me introduce myself. My name is Fisher. I'm very pleased to finally meet you, Rachel."

Indigo and three other men entered. The men took seats on the benches, while Indigo continued to the front of the room. "Where is everyone else, Pathik?"

Pathik eyed Fisher, though he spoke to Indigo. "They should be here soon. Nandy had to take the children to Saidon, who will watch them during the council meeting. Then she had to fetch Malgam."

As if on cue Nandy and Malgam appeared, and joined the group seated on the benches.

"Do you mind moving down a bit, Pathik?" Fisher moved to the end of the bench Pathik and Rachel were sitting on.

Pathik didn't move at all. "You don't want a place next to Michael today, Fisher? You seemed to think *that* was the best seat, last council meeting."

Fisher remained standing at the end of the bench, but his smile disappeared. "I stand by Michael every day, Pathik, as you know. I owe him that much."

Rachel felt like she was being squeezed. The two boys just stared at each other. Finally, she nudged Pathik. "Scoot down," she whispered.

Pathik dropped his eyes to Rachel. He sighed and moved over. Rachel scooted too and Fisher, grinning, took a seat next to her. Rachel turned her focus to Indigo at the front of the room. She refused to look at either Pathik or Fisher.

Nipper slunk into the room. He walked up the aisle casually and flopped down near Indigo's feet.

"Well," said Indigo, nodding toward the Woolly, "it looks like we can now begin." There was a low laugh from one of the men on the benches. Rachel turned to look; it was an imposing-looking man, with white hair grown well past his shoulders. He was missing his right arm.

"You laugh, Michael, but Nipper may be an important participant in our quest." Indigo motioned toward Nandy. "Nandy has an idea as to how he may help us rescue Daniel."

Nandy walked to the front of the room and spoke.

"You all know Malgam's gift." The men nodded. Pathik and Fisher nodded too. Rachel wanted to raise her hand and say she did not know Malgam's gift. Instead she jabbed Pathik with her elbow, and shot him a questioning look. She'd asked him on the trek to camp what his father's gift was, but he'd only told her what the name meant—a mixture, a combination of elements.

"Just listen," he said. He barely looked at her when he said it. But Nandy must have seen the look on Rachel's face. She smiled at her.

"Malgam can see from other people's eyes, Rachel. He can see what they see, as if he were looking at the same thing—as if his mind and their sight were intertwined."

Rachel nodded as though she understood, but she felt more confused than ever.

"Daniel knows Nipper," Nandy continued, addressing

all in the room. "If Nipper can get near enough for Daniel to see him, we think Daniel will know we're trying to rescue him. He'll put it together that Malgam could see for us, see what he's seeing. We think Daniel could give us enough visual information to help us get in and out of the Roberts' camp safely."

Michael shook his head. "You've already tried seeing through Daniel. You saw nothing but darkness. Why would we risk lives on a dead man?"

"I saw darkness, not emptiness, Michael. For all we know Daniel is drugged, or asleep." Malgam sounded angry. He looked at Rachel. "He is not dead. If someone is dead, I see emptiness. It's a different thing."

"Assuming that Daniel is not drugged, or sleeping, or anything worse once you got there, how would the Woolly know what you wanted?" Michael sounded skeptical.

"We have a game," said Nandy. "He plays *find it* often with me. He knows some names, like Malgam, and Pathik, and Daniel. He could find him. If Daniel's drugged, it won't do us much good, but if he sees Nipper he'll know we're near, and he'll give us what he can." Nandy ignored Michael's snort, and spoke to the rest of the assembly. "If Malgam still sees just darkness once we're there and we've tried this, we'll go in blind if we have to do it that way. But we're going."

Michael looked unimpressed.

Nandy wasn't so easily dismissed. "Find Michael, Nipper," she said, cocking her head at the Woolly.

Nipper tilted his head back, looking up at Nandy with an expression that could only be described as distaste.

"Yes, Nipper. I do mean Michael." Nandy was careful not to look anywhere but at the Woolly.

Nipper finally rose, as languidly as any being could. He swung his head toward Michael and lifted his chin, as though pointing. He looked back at Nandy.

"No, you have to actually go to him."

The Woolly might as well have rolled his eyes. But go to Michael he did. He padded down the aisle to where Michael sat, and stood before him, tail lashing.

"Humph." Michael barely glanced at Nipper. He turned to Indigo. "Who would go?"

"I will go," said Indigo. "Malgam, of course, and Nandy, so that Nipper might be more inclined to help us. Perhaps one other."

Pathik stood. "I'm going." He looked at Michael defiantly.

Fisher stood too. "And I will go," he said. He didn't look at Michael.

Michael made a disgusted sound. He turned to Malgam. "If Indigo insists upon going, then you must stay here. You can see from here. For both of you to go and risk death is foolish. We need the succession."

Malgam smiled at Michael, but there was impatience in his voice. "I *can* see from here. But will I let my father, my son . . . my *love*, go for my friend, and stay behind? For your *succession*?" He shook his head at Michael.

"We've discussed the succession enough." Indigo sounded annoyed. "You know it must be a camp decision."

"From the father to the son to the son to the son!" Michael snapped back at Indigo. "It has always been your blood leading us!"

"And it will lead on!" Indigo thundered. "*If* it is the will of the camp, *if* it is the will of my son." Michael began to speak, but Indigo shook his head and silenced him. "Times change, Michael. We must change too. For now, back to the matter at hand."

The rest of the council meeting was given to details: who would teach the children in Nandy's place, what would happen if any one of the rescue party was killed. Rachel listened dully until they got to that part, at which point she began to realize they were actually going to go someplace where one of them *might be killed*. She was both afraid and a little awestruck.

These people cared enough about her father to risk their lives for him. Rachel watched them talking, and remembered how she and her mother and Ms. Moore had talked in Ms. Moore's parlor back home on The Property, when they were planning how to help Pathik get the medicine he needed to save his father. The risk had been the same; Rachel understood that now in a way she hadn't then. Her mother and Ms. Moore, and Jonathan too, had risked their lives to help these people.

Rachel feared that the risk wasn't over for them either. She wondered where her mother was now. Was she making something for Ms. Moore in the kitchen of the main house? Was she on her way to Bensen for the weekly supply run? Had EOs swarmed The Property, tipped off by her old friend Peter? Was her mother in some cold, gray holding cell right now? Without warning, two tears slipped down Rachel's cheek. She swiped at her face and looked around, but nobody had noticed. She snuck a look at Pathik, but he was engrossed in the talk of preparations for the trek.

Rachel tried to listen, but she suddenly felt so tired. She just wanted to go lie down, but she wanted to lie down on her own little cot, in the bedroom of the guesthouse on The Property. She wanted to hear her mother making homey noises in the kitchen as she drifted off to sleep. She wanted everything to be like it was before, when her father was a dead hero, and her mother was a better-safe-than-sorry, overprotective nuisance, and the Others were just a fun, scary fascination she read about in net books.

CHAPTER 6

ELIZABETH PULLED THE greenhouse door closed and headed for the main house. She heard the low hum of the Enforcement vehicle before she saw it. By the time she reached the yard of the main house, the Enforcement Officers were already standing on the driveway. There were two, in the gray uniforms that for so many had come to symbolize terror. They weren't the same two who had come the night Rachel Crossed.

"Ms. Moore?" One of them blocked Elizabeth's path to the porch.

"Yes?" She didn't try to hide her irritation.

"Ms. Elizabeth Moore?" The second EO consulted his digitab, comparing her to some unseen data.

"Yes." Elizabeth sharpened the edge in her voice, hoping it would distract the EO from the beating of her heart—it felt like he must be able to see her chest move from where he stood.

"Do you provide Gainful Employment for a Vivian Quillen?"

"I do. Why?"

"We need to see her."

"She's . . ." Elizabeth tried to think of a viable lie, but the front door of the main house opened behind her before she could.

"Is there a problem, officers?" Vivian walked down the porch steps past the first EO and stood next to Elizabeth.

"Are you Vivian Quillen?" The EO with the digitab stroked the screen, then tapped it, and consulted the resulting display.

"I am." Vivian didn't look at Elizabeth.

The other EO stepped forward and took hold of Vivian's wrist. "We need you to come with us."

"For what reason, officer?" Elizabeth stepped closer to Vivian.

"It doesn't concern you." He took a pair of plasticuffs out and put them on her. Elizabeth started to say something, but the look on his face stopped her. He turned back to Vivian.

"We're taking you to the station in Bensen." He pushed her toward the Enforcement vehicle.

"I'll go with her, officers. Let me just get our coats and—"

The EO with the digitab stepped in front of Elizabeth. "You're staying here. Depending on how things go, she might be released tonight. If she's being detained, she can contact you from the station."

"It's fine, Elizabeth." Vivian smiled, but her face was ashen. "I'm sure there's some mix-up, that's all." She held Elizabeth's gaze, trying to convey something.

Elizabeth watched, helpless, as the EOs put Vivian in the back of their vehicle. Then they got in the front, faces grim, and drove away.

VIVIAN KEPT HER head down during the drive to Bensen. The EOs said nothing to her, and she said nothing to them. She just stared at the grate separating the back of the vehicle from the front. It was grimy from years of hands, and there was a dark brown stain on the lower right corner that looked suspiciously like blood. Vivian wondered how long it had been there. She tried not to imagine who had been sitting where she was now, bleeding.

The interrogation room at the Bensen station was empty except for two chairs and a small table. It was cold. They let Vivian sit in it alone for over an hour. When the door to the room finally opened, she had managed to remember most of the meditative techniques she had learned during her training as a collaborator, and she felt almost tranquil. She watched the man who had entered sit down across from her. She watched as he placed a slim case on the table. She studied his face the way she might have examined a dead rattlesnake, curious, but not alarmed.

The man didn't say anything for what seemed like a long time. He just looked back at her, silent. Vivian resisted the urge to speak; she knew his silence was designed to make her babble. She focused on his chin, a sharp chin, lasered to a hairless smoothness. He had a mole there, just left of center, in the shape of a heart. It was an interesting choice, to keep that mole. Nobody did anymore. Any sort of imperfection was easily erased at a laser clinic.

The man sighed, an exaggerated, overburdened sigh. Vivian kept her eyes on his mole. His hand appeared in her line of sight, fingers snapping briskly.

"Enough," he said.

She looked up, into his eyes. They looked empty.

"Do you know a Peter Hill?"

"Don't you have to read me a statement of my rights?"

The man slumped on one arm, holding his chin. "You are being interrogated on a matter of national security," he droned. "You have the right to humdy hum deed um dee hum. And also, lah de la dee lalala." He let the nonsense sounds rise and fall in pitch, like a little tune. Then he smiled brightly at her. "Happy now?" He looked maniacal at that moment, mad with power no human should have over another.

Vivian wasn't surprised at his actions. He was what she and her fellow collaborators had always been warned about.

Would she be returned to The Property? Or perhaps incarcerated in some holding center? Or would she never again see anything outside of the room she sat in now? She wondered where Rachel was at that very moment. She wondered if she was warm, and dry, and fed.

The man placed his hands on the case he had brought in, sliding them along its edges like some cheap jeweler at the annual fair in Bensen, about to reveal a very large, very fake gem inside. He pressed some hidden catch and a soft click sounded. The man raised the lid of the case, obscuring Vivian's view of the contents. His smile remained undiminished. Holding her gaze, he shifted the case so that it was sideways, allowing her to see inside.

The case was lined in deep blue velvet. There were four fitted compartments, a large one for a power-pack/handle, and three smaller ones for attachments. The handle was covered with what looked to Vivian like real black leather. It must have been fake, but it was a high quality fake. The attachments were steel, highly polished so that they gleamed. Vivian saw that two were cutters and the third was a cauterizer. They stopped the bleeding so you lived longer.

The man took a digitab from his pocket—the smallest one Vivian had ever seen. He tapped the screen a few times, read whatever he saw there.

"So." He didn't look up. "The facts: Peter Hill, collaborator. Jolie Hill, his wife, female child, presumably his daughter, both Identified not long ago in Bensen. Where"—he raised his eyebrows—"you happen to live."

Vivian didn't correct him. He knew she didn't live in town. He was just trying to get her started. She remembered her training again—once you *started* talking, it was easier to *keep* talking. Best to remain mute until you were compelled to speak. Vivian tried not to think about what that long-ago trainer had meant when he said "compelled."

"Mother and daughter confined. Or at least, that was the last report."

Meaning that Jolie and her daughter could be dead. Vivian kept her face neutral.

"Your own husband was Called to Serve years ago, correct? He helped out in that last big skirmish with Samarik, was killed in action, correct?"

Vivian nodded. She hoped her face hadn't changed, hadn't revealed the pain she still felt, like her heart was being tugged from her chest—Daniel, dead. Killed in action, certainly, but not the kind of action this man cited. Vivian knew the Call to Serve had been a sham, just as Daniel had known. But he had to go; he had no choice.

"Peter Hill was a friend of your late husband's." It wasn't a question. "And of yours. And now he's disappeared." The man tilted his head at Vivian. "Did you know that?"

Vivian shook her head.

"Yes. His house is quite deserted. So strange that he would just . . . disappear, so soon after he visited you at your employer's home." The man reached into the case and plucked a tiny piece of lint from the velvet lining.

"That night, the night Peter visited you, that was the very same night your daughter ran away, wasn't it?"

Vivian nodded, and tried not to look at the case.

"So upsetting, I'm sure." The man waited. He reached into the case again, and stroked one of the cutter attachments.

He leaned forward to look at it, picked it up to examine a smudge. He rubbed his thumb over the smudge until it was gone.

Vivian kept seeing flashes of a memory, so long ago now. A young woman, a collaborator, being carried into the safe house by two men, one of them Daniel. They'd found her dumped by the side of the road. She was still making some noise, but not much. There was so little blood, but everywhere—her arms, her legs, her face, her abdomen where it showed through her ripped clothing—there were cauterized wounds; angry red lines or wider, circular areas, burned closed with a laser. Vivian started to go for the medical student they counted among their ranks, but Daniel shook his head. He went to the chest they kept in a cupboard, a chest none of the trainees liked to think about. Daniel took it out and removed a tiny paper envelope from it, one of several. He was careful to touch only the corner. He carried the envelope to the girl, who was lying on a cot, being tended to by three other trainees.

"Tessa." Daniel spoke the girl's name. She was in the same upper-level philosophy course he and Vivian were taking that semester at college. She opened her eyes and saw what he held. Her whimpering stopped. Slowly, she reached out toward him, her hand shaking.

"No, Daniel." One of the other trainees reached for Tessa's hand, but she slapped him away. She crooked her fingers at Daniel. He stepped closer and helped her grasp the paper envelope, steadying her hand.

"Can you wait a bit?" Daniel stroked her hair back from her forehead. Tessa shook her head frantically.

"Do you want us to stay?"

Tessa hesitated, then nodded. Daniel nodded too.

"We'll be right here with you, Tessa. Right here."

Tessa fumbled with the envelope. Her hands were shaking too hard to open it. One of the trainees moved to help, but Daniel stopped him.

"You can't touch the wafer—it's transdermal."

"She can't do it by herself."

"Tessa," Daniel said. He waited until her eyes were focused on him. "You can just eat the whole thing—the envelope is just rice paper. It will dissolve along with the wafer."

Tessa was taking very deep breaths now, practically gasping. She reached toward Daniel with the hand holding the tiny packet. He knelt next to her and took her wrist. He asked the question with his eyes. Tessa nodded, and Daniel helped guide her hand toward her mouth. She was shaking so hard she almost dropped it, but finally it rested on her tongue. She closed her mouth and smiled weakly at them all. Within moments she was gone.

"So you've had no news from her." The man's voice interrupted Vivian's reverie.

"Sorry?" She spoke before she thought.

"You've heard nothing," he said, enunciating each word. "From Rachel?" He looked impatient. "Your daughter?"

"No. I've heard nothing. I'd hoped . . ." Vivian let her thought remain unfinished.

"Yes?" The man twirled the cutter in his hand.

"I'd hoped she would get over her teenage fuss and come home, but I'm afraid something's happened to her now." Vivian carefully injected what she hoped was a realistic note of panic into her voice. "Since her father died it's been a huge struggle, and the EOs won't even look for her. Can't you get them to look, sir? Can't you help me?"

The man drew back, as if he feared she might try to touch him. He placed the cutter carefully back in its velvet hollow.

"Surely you have some power?" She tried for a whine.

The man scowled, glanced at his digitab. He considered her for another moment, but it was clear he'd moved on. He sighed, and snapped the case before him closed.

"Ms. Quillen," he said. "Vivian." He spoke very softly. "It would be best if you didn't travel outside the county. Actually, why don't you limit yourself to your place of employ and Bensen. We may want to talk with you further. And if you see Peter Hill, you are to report it immediately, Vivian. Do you understand?"

"But what about my Rachel?" Now Vivian didn't have to feign her tears. "Couldn't you please just send out a patrol? Just one?" When the man rose to leave she reached for him across the table. He flicked her hands away as though they were filthy.

"You should just be happy you're going home, Ms. Quillen." At the door he paused. He pointed a finger at his temple. "Don't think we won't be watching."

Vivian buried her head in her arms and sobbed.

CHAPTER 7

AFTER THE COUNCIL meeting Nandy and Rachel walked back to the hut together.

"You and I will be sleeping in there for now." Nandy jutted her chin toward one of the two doorways off the main room of the hut. "The boys will bunk in the other room." Nandy took some plates from a shelf on the wall and put them on the table. "Would you set these out for me, Rachel? Just us three tonight. Indigo and Malgam will be late—they have arrangements to make about who will do what while we're gone, and what happens if we don't . . . come back. And then they have to get Malgam's things from the hospital. They'll eat with some of the council, probably. Pathik should be here soon, though—he's probably off getting more wood."

"The hospital? Is that what you call that building where Malgam was?" Rachel placed the plates carefully; they were pottery, faded and chipped around the edges. She tried not to dwell on what Nandy had said about not coming back.

"That's what we use it for." Nandy handed Rachel three forks. "If someone gets sick we quarantine right away—we can't afford to have any sort of outbreak. The medicines we have aren't strong enough to fight the serious sicknesses." Nandy shrugged. "Malgam would have died without your antibiotics. Many have before him."

Rachel thought about this. She knew that Indigo had Crossed decades before. That was how he had met Ms. Moore; how they had fallen in love and had a baby—who turned out to be Malgam. But if Others had Crossed since then, wouldn't they have at least some medications from the other side? Had no Other Crossed since Indigo? She started to pose the question, but it must have been written on her face.

"We don't Cross anymore." Nandy had been watching her puzzle things out. "We don't have any keys." She added three cups to the table setting. "You know about Indigo's time over there." It wasn't a question.

"I know he Crossed." Rachel tried to remember all that Ms. Moore had told her and Vivian that night in the parlor, when everything changed. "He Crossed with friends of his—they were on a mission, though Ms. Moore never said what it was about. She said they each had more than one key to disable the Line."

"They did. They had three each, actually, according to the story we're told. Keys passed down from father to son, and nobody knows for certain how we came to be in possession of them. There are lots of stories. Some say a high-ranking Reg got them over right before the Line was activated.

"But Indigo's trek used the last of the supply. Since then, some have tried to figure out how to make keys. My own father tried—cobbled together prototypes from bits and pieces gathered and saved over decades, following notes from his father, and ideas from his father's father, about how the Line might work."

"How *does* it work?"

Nandy chuckled. "I don't know," she said. "It has something to do with energy fields, but I don't understand it. My great-grandfather scribbled some notes that were passed down through my family, notes that looked like some sort of mathematic code but that must have meant something. My grandfather only learned that energy fields were involved by accident." She grinned. "I'm told he was quite the rebel—he was supposed to be on sentry duty, but instead he was testing the Line. He wasn't supposed to be anywhere near it—none of us are. But he was right next to it, pushing on it, and there was a lightning strike. He fell right through to the other side. Thankfully, he Crossed right back before the effect was over. Otherwise he would have been stuck over there." Nandy took one of the oil jars that lit the interior of the hut and ignited some shavings in the fireplace. She added twigs and then three logs from a small stack next to the hearth.

Rachel thought of her own experience trying to Cross

the Line. It seemed so long ago that she had dared herself to try. She still remembered the soft, firm resistance of it. And how much that silly, little-girl stunt had changed her life.

"That must be what they mean by a Crossing Storm," she said.

"What do you know of them?" Nandy looked up from where she was cracking small blue eggs into an old iron pan.

"Some of the net books talk about Crossing Storms, where the storm somehow makes it possible for the Others . . . I mean for you people, I mean . . . I mean for people like you . . ." Rachel stopped talking. Nothing she said sounded like what she meant.

"You mean for people like us, whose great-grandparents were separated from their lovers and daughters and sons, with no warning and no remorse; people like us, who got abandoned over here, who got left to suffer and die when the bombs went off, who got left to *die* here, by people like you?" Nandy stared at Rachel, something wild in her eyes.

Rachel stared back. "No," she said quietly.

"No, *what*?" Nandy sounded more angry than Rachel had heard her, more angry than she had thought it possible for Nandy to be, really.

"No," Rachel whispered, looking straight into Nandy's eyes. "*Not* by people like me. People like me wouldn't do that. *I* didn't do that. I never would." She walked to the corner where her bag and duffel were and stood looking down at them. She felt tears stinging her eyes, but she didn't cry. She wanted to take her things and go. She wanted to go find her father herself, without any help from this woman, without any help from anyone. She wanted to find him and look at him and hug him and hear him say he loved her and that everything would be all right. But the most she could do right now was to go outside and sit, and wait for the moment to change. She fumbled in her pack for some gloves.

"Rachel."

Rachel didn't turn. She felt her cheeks burning. She kept looking for the gloves.

"Rachel." Nandy touched her shoulder, turned her around. Her face was etched with regret. "I'm so sorry." She looked at Rachel and her eyes looked helpless. She shook her head. "I just get so angry, and I have nowhere to put it. I'm so angry at what they did. Every time one of us dies because of a simple infection, or in childbirth . . . What they did goes on and on for us. And they don't care at all. But you're right. You are not them. You had nothing to do with it."

Rachel just looked at her. She didn't know what to say.

"Come help me with dinner?" Nandy smiled a small, tentative smile.

Rachel nodded. She followed Nandy to the hearth. Nandy handed her a smooth piece of clean wood, carved with a wider, paddle-like end.

"If you could stir those up." Nandy nodded to the eggs.

Rachel saw three tiny yolks floating in the pan. She broke them with the utensil and began to stir.

"Where did these come from?"

Nandy looked up from the table, where she was measuring some sort of rough flour from a crock. "They're from a bird that lives in our woods—a funny bird that can't fly. They lay three eggs at a time, and we gather one from each nest." She stopped her measuring and leaned on the table. She waited until Rachel noticed the silence and looked back.

"I truly am sorry, Rachel."

"It's okay." It was Rachel's turn to smile a tentative smile. "I'd be mad too."

They worked in silence for a few minutes. But Rachel had so many questions racing through her mind that she couldn't stay quiet for long.

"I met Fisher today. Before the council meeting. Pathik didn't seem to like him."

"Oh, there's lots of history there." Nandy shrugged. "I do wish those boys would loosen up a bit. It's all about their fathers. Well, not fathers—I mean, Malgam is Pathik's father, but Michael isn't Fisher's. He's his guardian." Nandy took a bit more flour from the crock. "Fisher's parents were both killed when he was four. Michael took him in, and raised him up like his own son. And Michael and Malgam don't always get along. So the boys get torn apart a bit with that."

"How did Fisher's parents die?" Rachel knew what it was like to lose one parent—she couldn't imagine losing both.

Nandy shrugged again. "We don't really know. Could have been a forest creature. Could have been the Roberts. We never found their bodies. They just didn't come back from gathering wood one day."

"Why do you and the Roberts live in different camps? Why don't you work together? It seems so hard here, without having to worry about your own people being enemies."

Nandy dumped the flour into a bowl and added some oil. She began to mix the two together.

"The Roberts don't think of us as people." She sighed. "A long time ago, when the first gifts started to show in children, a man named Robert was one of the leaders. He thought the gifts were signs of evil. He thought all the children who had them should be killed. Indigo's grandfather was another leader at that time. He wouldn't allow any children to be killed. He said that all of us were people, that all of us were good, gift or no gift. So there was a split. Some of our people went with Robert—"

The hut door burst open in what seemed to be Pathik's usual fashion. He came inside, his arms filled with wood for the fire, but he was halted by Nandy's scowl. She was looking at the floor, where the rag they used to stuff the crack in the ill-fitting door lay, fallen when Pathik opened the door.

Pathik raised his eyebrows as far as they would go and shrugged. He set the wood down on the hearth and returned to the door, picking the rag up and carefully dusting it off before he stuffed it in the crack. Nandy shook her head, but then she started to laugh.

"That door!"

"Bet I have something to fix it." Rachel hurried to her duffel bag. She rummaged in it and came up with a small case. Pathik nodded; he recognized it. He'd seen some of what Ms. Moore had packed in the duffel when they were still on the way to base camp. Since they had arrived there had been little time; Pathik had loaded the batteries into the solar charger and put it on the roof of the hospital to catch light, but there had been no time to try out the tools and other items.

"What is it?" Nandy came to get a better look.

"It's a laser saw."

"I'll go get the batteries." Pathik looked excited. He had been fascinated by the assortment of tools and other items Ms. Moore had sent. He'd grilled Rachel endlessly during the trek to camp about how her life was: what did she eat, how was it cooked, what sort of vehicles were there. Rachel had been exhausted with all his questions.

"Batteries? Too bad. Those run out of energy, right?" Nandy touched the case. "They'll end up in the tech cemetery."

"The tech cemetery?" Rachel wondered what that meant.

Nandy nodded. "You should have Pathik show you sometime."

"These are solar charged—Ms. Moore packed lots of things that run off of them," said Rachel. "She also packed a solar array that will let us recharge them. Pathik put it up on the roof of one of the buildings, so it could catch the sun. I think this will trim that metal so the door fits right." Rachel snapped open the case and took out a folded piece of paper that lay atop the tool. She handed it to Nandy. "Directions."

Pathik came back, out of breath. He held three slim

rectangular objects. "Is this enough of them? I thought I remembered it taking two." He and Rachel had read the directions on the trek to camp.

"Yes, I think it's two." Rachel removed the laser saw from the case. It was rectangular too, palm-sized, with an opening on one end and a dial on the side.

"So you snap that off," said Nandy, pointing to the end with no opening. Rachel frowned at it. She couldn't see anything to snap off, and she didn't remember what the directions had said.

"May I?" Nandy reached for the tool.

Rachel handed it to her.

Nandy snapped off the end of the tool, revealing two slots where the batteries slid in. She took two of them from Pathik and pushed them into the slots until they clicked. Then she snapped the end piece back on.

"And this is the controller." Nandy pressed the dial on the side and a light shot out of the end with the opening.

"Careful!" Rachel reached over and pressed the dial again to turn the light off. "That can cut through metal." Rachel *did* remember that part. She'd watched Jonathan use a similar tool back at the greenhouse, and she remembered his warning about how dangerous the laser beam could be.

Nandy looked doubtful. She handed the laser to Rachel.

"Well?" Nandy pointed to the door and tapped her foot with mock impatience.

Rachel grinned. "Can you hold it closed, Pathik?"

Once the door was closed fast against the frame, it was

clear where the metal edge was too large. Rachel pressed
the dial on the laser saw and adjusted the light until it was
the thinnest beam she could get. Then she traced it along the
metal. It left a tiny black line where it touched. When Rachel
reached the end of the ill-fitted area she turned the laser saw
off. All three of them peered at the door.

"Hmmm." Nandy looked unimpressed. Pathik reached
to touch the metal. At the slightest pressure, there was a
clinking sound, and the piece Rachel had trimmed fell to
the floor. Nandy and Pathik stared down at it openmouthed.
Nandy reached down and picked it up, looking first at it and
then at the door. Pathik pushed the door snug shut.

"Fits perfect," he said. He waved his hand back and forth
where the rag had always been stuffed in the gap. "No cold
breeze, Nandy."

Nandy ran her own hand over the spot. A slow smile
spread across her face. "I guess you'll have to find some
other thing to get scolded for now, Pathik." She turned to
Rachel. "Thank you. That draft may not seem like much to
you, but it's driven me crazy. It gets cold in the winter!"

"You're very welcome." Rachel packed the saw back into
the duffel. "Pathik, Nandy said you have a tech cemetery."

"Go show her, Pathik—we have time before the food
is ready." Nandy shrugged. "Who knows, maybe she'll see
something we could be using."

Pathik led her outside, and they walked to the far side of
the camp, behind the larger buildings. There was a clearing
there, and in it was a huge pile of junk. As they got closer,

Rachel could see why Nandy called it a tech cemetery. It was a pile of modern technology—though far from what Rachel thought of as modern. Antique-looking streamer carcasses were thrown in a heap, monitors cracked, wires trailing from some. There were other things too, all things that would have required electricity, or a signal, or a broadcast, to be of any use.

"Who put it all here?" Rachel saw a half-buried keyboard at her feet. She scuffed at the dirt, uncovering lettered keys.

"I don't know. Someone from when it first happened. After they figured out we couldn't use any of it anymore."

"Why do you keep it?"

Pathik stared at the pile. "Why not?" He shoved his hands in his pockets. "Maybe we'll need something, someday. Maybe something will make some sort of difference. Anyway, it's probably time to eat. Let's go."

Rachel looked back at the pile as they left. It didn't look to her like anything there would ever make any sort of difference.

They had a simple dinner of eggs and a flat bread Nandy made out of flour and water and oil. There was water to drink and for dessert, an odd sort of dried fruit that reminded Rachel of apples. The interior of the hut was dim, since there were no windows, but the fire gave off a homey glow, and its warmth made Rachel sleepy.

By the time Malgam and Indigo arrived it was early evening. Much fuss was made over the repaired door, and over Malgam's improved color too. But some part of the lighthearted talk seemed forced. The prospect of the next day's journey was like another person in the room—a surly, unlikeable person at that.

"Well, I suggest we all get some sleep." Malgam rose and stretched. "We'll need it tomorrow morning."

Nandy rose too. She gave each of the men a hug, and then Pathik. "We're in there, Rachel," she said, indicating the room she had earlier. Rachel began to follow her into the room.

"Here now!" Indigo's voice was a soft thunder. "Do we not get hugs from you too, Rachel?" He was smiling at her when she turned.

She smiled back, and went to him. His hug felt the way she'd imagined a grandfather's hug might feel; gentle and warm and safe. She wished she could stay there and hug him for longer. She went to Malgam next, and his hug was awkward, but kind. He grinned at her and tousled her hair.

"Sleep well, Rachel, and many thanks again, for your help."

Then it was Pathik's turn. He looked as uncomfortable as a person could look without being in actual pain. She held out her arms, and he held out his, but they didn't move toward each other. They stood like that for the longest moment, two feet apart, eyes avoiding eyes, until Malgam finally stuttered out a laugh.

"Awww, just shake hands, my loves. We're all tired."

Rachel dropped one of her arms, and reached out her hand. But Pathik shot his father a look, and stepped toward her. He took her outstretched hand in one of his, put his other hand around her waist, and led her in a playful dance, smiling. Then he wrapped his arms around her and held her, careful and soft, for just a moment.

"Sleep well," he said, low, and she could feel his breath in her ear.

Later that night, lying in the darkness, listening to Nandy's slow, even breaths, Rachel thought she could still feel the tickle of Pathik's whisper.

CHAPTER 8

THEY HAD PLANNED to start at first light, but Rachel was awakened long before that. She heard Indigo's voice coming from the main room.

"Bring him here. Be certain he has no weapons."

Nandy was sitting up in her bed, listening too. She looked at Rachel.

"Let's go."

Neither had undressed completely the night before; Nandy had said they would need to be ready to go quickly, so they had kept all but jackets and shoes on. In two minutes they were out of bed and in the hut's main room.

Indigo and Malgam were seated at the table. Pathik was lighting oil jars. The room was chilly; the fire had died during the night and they wouldn't be building one this morning—they planned to be gone soon. Nandy sent a questioning look to Malgam.

"The far-station sentries found a man wandering. He

says he's looking for you, Rachel." Malgam sounded irritated.

"It must be Jonathan!" Rachel sat down hard; she felt oddly dizzy. Jonathan. Here, in the camp.

"Rachel." Nandy knelt in front of her. "Who is Jonathan? Are you afraid he'll hurt you?" She touched Rachel's cheek gently, tucked a tendril of hair behind her ear. "We won't let anyone hurt you if we can stop them, Rachel."

Rachel smiled, and shook her head.

"He's my friend. He works for Ms. Moore on The Property. He's always watched out for me."

There was a soft knock on the door.

"Enter." Indigo and Malgam rose from their chairs. Rachel stood too, and hastily swiped at her hair. She knew she must look a mess.

The door opened, and two men entered, holding a third by his arms. Rachel was about to protest, to tell them to let Jonathan go, when she saw the third man's face. She took a step back, and toppled right into Pathik, who was still standing behind her. He caught her.

"What's wrong?" He whispered in her ear, holding her steady against him.

Rachel didn't take her eyes off of the man. "It's not Jonathan," she whispered back. She felt Pathik's arms tighten around her. Then he released her, and moved to her side. Indigo, who had been watching the man, turned and noticed Rachel's face. After a moment's deliberation he stepped in front of her, blocking the man's view of her. Rachel peeked cautiously past him.

"Who are you?" Indigo waited for the man to speak.

The man looked tired. There were streaks of dirt on his face, and there were dark circles under his eyes.

"Like I told your men, I'm part of the collaboration. Do you know about the collaboration?" The man looked from Indigo to Malgam. "I'm not here to cause any trouble."

"The sentries say you were asking about a girl. A girl from *your* side." Malgam crossed his arms and stared coldly.

"Yes." The man appraised Malgam. He didn't seem overly impressed. "I need to find her. She may have documents that are crucial to the collaboration."

"I'm told that the government doesn't let just anyone Cross. Why would they let a girl?" Malgam lifted his chin and looked down his nose at the man. "How," he asked, "did you Cross?"

Rachel reached out without looking away from the man and found Pathik's hand. She took hold of it and squeezed hard. Pathik squeezed back, but he too kept his eyes on the man.

"I had a key."

"Traitor!" Rachel let go of Pathik's hand and pushed past Indigo to stand in front of the man. "Liar!" Her face was red, her fists clenched at her sides, and she was shaking. It took everything she had to hold back from leaping on the man and tearing at him.

The man stared, stunned by her fury.

Rachel stared back. She seemed to be unaware of any

other person in the room. Pathik went to her and carefully touched her shoulder.

"Rachel." He turned her toward him and she moved stiffly, like a mannequin. "Is he Peter? The man you told me about?"

Rachel tore her eyes from the man, to meet Pathik's. She nodded.

"Who else could he be?" Rachel had never actually seen Peter, but this man knew her name. He knew she had the maps. It *had* to be Peter.

Pathik looked at the man.

"Are you Peter?"

The man nodded, relieved.

"Yes. I'm Rachel's mother's friend."

"Friend," spat Rachel, her lip curled in disgust. "You're no friend of my mother's. Though she thought you were." She turned away from him, to the Others.

"This man betrayed my mother when she asked for help. He called the EOs and led them to Ms. Moore's the night we had to Cross. He's the reason I had to Cross at all. We planned to use his key to disable the Line just long enough to put the medicine and other supplies on the other side. That way Pathik could get them and go." Rachel glared at Peter again, as if she could hurt him with her eyes. "You said you had a key. You said you'd bring it to us."

Peter shook his head. "I never called the EOs. They must have flagged me, Rachel. They followed me there, to that house where your mother was. I never planned to hurt her, or you."

Rachel shook her head. "You're lying. You wanted to trade my mother for your wife and daughter." She walked away, back to the table, where she sat with her back to the room. Pathik remained where he was, eyeing Peter.

"Did you use your key to Cross? The key you promised to bring to Rachel and her mother?" Pathik looked disgusted.

Peter shook his head again. He raised his hands, palms up, in front of him. "I had the key in my pocket that night. But Vivian said Rachel had run away. She didn't want the key anymore. I did want the maps, because I thought that I might be able to use them to bargain with the government—they took my wife and my child. That's the only thing I wanted from your mom, Rachel. And when she told me that you had them with you, I was frantic. I guessed that you must have Crossed somehow when the EOs couldn't scan your genid that night. If you'd really just run away, they would have picked you up on a scan."

"What maps? What are you talking about?" Indigo had moved forward to stand next to Pathik.

"Daniel—Rachel's father—was given some maps to protect, maps that are very valuable to the collaboration. When he died—"

"My father's alive." Rachel shifted in her seat, so that she could see Peter's face. She felt some small satisfaction when it drained of color.

"What do you mean, alive?" Peter looked astonished. His tone made Rachel look at him more carefully. She studied him, trying to find a false note that would reveal his deceit, but it really did seem to her that Peter sounded genuinely . . . hopeful.

THEY QUESTIONED PETER thoroughly. He managed to convince Indigo and Malgam, at least, that he intended no treachery. Rachel wasn't so sure. Finally, Malgam took Peter off to find him some clean clothes and some food. They had decided to allow him, after much pleading, to come on the rescue mission. There were only a few hours left until they had to set out.

"He wasn't lying, at least not that I could feel." Pathik looked almost apologetic; he knew Rachel believed Peter was lying. But he'd been searching the man's emotions as he told his story, and his gift told him otherwise.

"Maybe there really was a misunderstanding," said Indigo. "We'll watch him closely. For now, I think we'd all better go back to bed."

As Rachel turned to go to the room she had been sharing with Nandy, he spoke her name.

"Stay with me for a bit, Rachel." Indigo sat at the table and motioned for her to join him

As she sat down, Rachel noticed a small vase on the table, next to the oil lamp. It hadn't been there when she went to sleep. It held a flower, a flower that drew her to it like a magnet, because it was an orchid.

"Where did this come from?"

"I picked it." Indigo smiled at Rachel's expression. "We have wild ones here, Rachel. At least, we do now."

Rachel gently touched a velvet petal. "When I was working for Ms. Moore I read about varieties that could grow in fairly harsh conditions. This one is not like any I've seen before—" Rachel looked at Indigo. "What do you mean, *now*?"

"We never had orchids here. I brought some with me when I came back. She . . . Elizabeth sent them with me. I had to work pretty hard to get them to naturalize, but they did." He admired the flower—a deep, red-black lady slipper shape. "They are quite lovely in their own strange way, aren't they?"

"They are." Rachel wondered where the orchids grew here. She wanted to see them.

"Rachel, what are these maps that Peter talked about? Do you know?"

"Yes. Well, no. I know that they are maps of some sort, but they don't really look like any maps I've seen before. They look more like sets of specifications, or something. All I really know is that my mother told me to keep them safe."

"And do you feel like they are? Safe?"

Rachel thought about where the maps were, tucked away in her bag. She nodded at Indigo. She wondered to herself if she should move them someplace else.

"Good enough." Indigo smiled at her. "You should probably get some rest now. We leave very soon."

INDIGO SAT ADMIRING the orchid blossom long after Rachel had left the room. He too reached out to touch the tender bloom. Funny how something as simple as a flower could bring a certain grace to this rough existence. Elizabeth had helped him see that beauty came in all forms, and showed him its transformative powers. He'd tried hard to integrate that into his life since he'd come back. He knew he'd failed, in comparison to what she could have done.

He reached into his pocket and took out the envelope he had been carrying since Rachel gave it to him. He looked at his name again, written in her hand, and then he ripped it open.

> *Indigo,*
> *I should have come with you. I know that now.*
> *I'm so sorry.*
> > *Elizabeth*

Indigo smiled. That was so like her. To know that very little needed to be said in order to say it all.

I know that now. Those four words made him sad. What must she be suffering, knowing that she had made the wrong decision all those years ago? Knowing that she couldn't change her mind. He had known immediately what they had found in each other. She had too, but . . .

Indigo crumpled the letter in his hand. But *what?* But she was too young? Too inexperienced? Too cowardly. He hated it when he thought of her that way, but sometimes, he couldn't help it. They could have been together, all these years. And his son might not be so hard, so ready to believe that people couldn't be trusted. He'd tried many times to explain to Malgam that a mother's lack of courage didn't mean a lack of love, but even he didn't really believe that. It was something he struggled with often. He knew Elizabeth had loved Malgam. He'd seen it in her eyes when she held him. But that love hadn't given her the courage to Cross. She'd let her son grow up motherless, far from her, because of her own fears.

His sour mood didn't last. After a few minutes he smoothed the letter and fitted it back into its envelope. Then, he rose stiffly from the table and took himself to bed.

CHAPTER 9

THEY MADE GOOD progress the first day. The weather was brisk but dry, and the forest seemed almost friendly. Malgam and Daniel took turns leading the group. Rachel walked with Pathik most of the time, though Fisher dropped back to walk with them often, which seemed to irritate Pathik. When Fisher went ahead to talk to Malgam, Rachel questioned Pathik.

"Why are you being so touchy with Fisher?"

"What do you mean, touchy?"

"Every time he comes back to walk with us you act like he's contagious."

Pathik scowled. "He's not coming back to walk with *us*."

"What do you mean?"

Pathik just shook his head. "Fisher always has plans." Then he was off, heading for the front of the group.

When Fisher saw Pathik leave Rachel's side he dropped back.

"Problems in romance land?"

Rachel felt her face get hot. She stopped walking for a moment, but Nandy and Indigo were close behind them. "I don't know what you're talking about," she sputtered.

"Really?" Fisher cocked his head and grinned. "You seem awfully upset. I just thought maybe the romance had—"

"There's no romance."

"Ah." Fisher walked in silence for a bit. "Are you sure?"

"Of course I'm sure."

"Hmm." Fisher watched her from the corners of his eyes. "I just thought there might be."

"Well, there's not." She wouldn't look at him.

"Does Pathik know that?"

"Of course he does."

Fisher walked with her for the rest of that day's trek. He was pleasant enough, but Rachel kept trying to catch Pathik's eye. He was up front, walking with Malgam and Peter, and when he looked back he didn't seem to notice her.

It was easy to tell when they were getting close to the Roberts' camp. They began to see refuse—ragged pieces of plastic tarp, filthy, rooted scraps of cloth, what was left of the rib cage of some animal—strewn in the underbrush. They passed the rusted remains of some sort of vehicle, resting on its side as though it had been tossed there. It was barely recognizable; it had no doors or windows; all that was left of the interior was a skeletal framework of springs and supports, covered with ivy.

Pathik went ahead to scout the area. Rachel saw him

leave, and he didn't look back at her when he did. When they were close enough to detect a stench hanging in the air, Indigo called a halt.

"It will be nightfall soon. We need to find a place we can defend and set camp."

"There's a huge boulder just ahead." Pathik appeared as if on cue. "We could camp at its base and have cover on one side, at least." His cheeks were flushed from moving quickly through the forest. Rachel felt her own cheeks flush to match, just from hearing his voice. She felt her shoulders relax and realized she had been tense since he left to scout ahead.

Indigo nodded. "That sounds good. Anything else?"

"The stink doesn't get any better." Pathik wrinkled his nose. "I think they just dump their waste pots a ways from their camp instead of properly burying them. I didn't sense any guards. They may be closer to the camp."

"Let's make for the boulder, then. Good work, Pathik." Indigo began to walk, and the others followed. Pathik waited until Rachel and Fisher reached him and fell in beside them. He kept his eyes on the ground.

The boulder *was* huge. Taller than two men and twice as wide, it was a gray, lichened hulk, crouching on the forest floor. There was a natural clearing around it, as though over the decades no sapling had dared grow too near.

They set up camp for the night.

"We should do it before dark, so I can still see what Daniel sees," said Malgam.

Nipper was sitting quietly a few feet away, where he had

been watching them set up the camp. Nandy called softly to him. He considered her for a moment, then glided to her side. She reached out to stroke him and he closed his eyes, leaning in toward her.

"Nipper, we need to find Daniel. Can you find him? Find Daniel?"

The Woolly opened one eye a slit, and pushed his head harder against Nandy's hand. He growled low in his throat.

"He doesn't know what you're saying." Malgam's tone was a mixture of scorn and regret. "It's too much to expect he would understand what you want, all the way out here in unfamiliar surroundings." He sighed. "I don't know what we were thinking. He isn't even *that* good at the game back home."

The low growl became stronger and Nipper's other eye opened. He turned both of his eyes on Malgam in a baleful glare.

Nandy smiled. "Oh, I think he has quite a clear idea of what I'm asking. Don't you, Nipper?" She scratched Nipper's neck. "We really need to find Daniel, Nips. Can you go find him now? Please?"

Nipper fell silent. He turned away from Malgam, clearly dismissing him as insignificant. He pushed his head against Nandy's shoulder and snuffled her ear. Then he sat back and looked at her.

"Hemmmm," said Nipper, his expression conveying a question.

Nandy nodded. "I know. But we need to find out."

Without another sound, Nipper turned and walked away.

"Be careful, Nipper." Nandy sounded worried. Rachel scooted closer and put her arm around Nandy's shoulders. Everyone watched the Woolly disappear into the brush.

"At least he's going in the right direction." Malgam shrugged. Nandy threw her bedroll at him.

"Shush your mouth." She glared at Malgam almost as fiercely as Nipper had, even though she knew he was teasing her.

"He'll be okay," said Malgam. "The Roberts won't know him as anything but a Woolly, assuming they manage to catch a glimpse of him."

"Let's hope Daniel manages to catch a glimpse of him." Nandy rose and retrieved the bedroll she had thrown. "Rachel, let's get our beds laid out. By the time we've done that, Nipper should be at their camp."

Rachel untied her own bedroll. She whispered to Nandy. "Did he say something to you?"

"Who?" Nandy was clearing small rocks from the area she planned to put her bedroll out on.

"Nipper. When you asked him to go, he . . . he said something. And then you said 'I know,' like you were answering him." Rachel felt a little foolish.

Nandy smoothed her bed and patted a spot next to her. Rachel sat down.

"He doesn't talk to me, not in that way." Nandy smiled. "But I've known Nipper his whole life." She spoke softly, so Malgam wouldn't be disturbed. "When he was just a tiny cub, he got separated from his mother somehow. She was probably killed by some other animal. And I found him, while I was out hunting eggs. He was half dead, standing on wobbly legs, weak from hunger. He should have bitten me the minute I touched him—I told you how vicious Woollies are—but he didn't. He didn't even growl. He just watched me come, and I could tell he was thinking. I could tell he knew he was out of options. And so he let me help him. And over the years we've learned how to communicate in a way, like you would with anyone, really."

"Does he love you? For saving him?"

Nandy shook her head. "I don't know, Rachel. I don't know if Woollies can love, at least the way you mean it. Malgam thinks they can't. Most people think they can't. All I know is that I love him. I get some grief for it, because there's not much time for that sort of thing out here. But I do love him. And I like to think that if he can, he loves me too." Nandy looked toward Malgam. "We'd best be quiet now, in case he's getting close."

Rachel watched Malgam. Nothing seemed to be happening; he betrayed no indication that he was seeing through another person's eyes, no twitching, no trance-like visage, no stiffened body, as though he were possessed by some other consciousness. She looked a question at Nandy.

"It might be a while," said Nandy. "We don't really know how far Nipper has to go, or how hard it might be for him to find Daniel if Daniel is actually . . ." Nandy didn't finish the sentence, but Rachel knew what she meant. They could have come all this way for nothing. Even though Malgam insisted he hadn't been dead last time Malgam tried to see through his eyes, Daniel could be dead now.

They waited, everyone quiet as the light faded more and more.

When it finally happened, it was less dramatic than Rachel had imagined it might be. Malgam began to nod, slowly at first, then rapidly. Nandy dropped down next to him, motioning Rachel over.

"He saw Nipper." Malgam was smiling. "It *is* Daniel, and he saw Nipper. I'm seeing . . . bars." Malgam's smile was replaced by a frown. "He's looking at one place on them . . . wait, now he's looking out through them. I see . . . ah, only one man."

"What man?" Rachel watched Malgam's face, trying to solve the puzzle on it. Nandy shook her head and held a finger to her lips.

"He's got to concentrate. We'll know soon enough. Just remember what he says even if it makes no sense. Sometimes it helps him later."

"Just one man, close by. The back of it is solid, rocks, maybe? But the front and the sides are the bars. Back to that place on the bars, he keeps going back to it . . . a lock! A lock of some sort." Malgam paused. "The campfire is far off. He isn't in the main camp. Somewhere off a ways. He . . ." Malgam grimaced. He was silent for a long time. When he spoke again, he looked at Nandy, not at Rachel.

"It's a dirt floor, where they keep him. He wrote in the dirt with a stick. His hands . . . he had a lot of trouble holding the stick. One of his hands is . . . broken."

Rachel tried not to think about what Malgam had just said. She took a deep breath, and another. She straightened her shoulders. She remembered in that moment how many times she had seen her mother do the same thing, how she would gather herself and face whatever was coming.

"What did he write?"

Malgam finally looked at her. His face was pale, drained.

"He wrote *Don't try it.*"

Rachel stared back at Malgam. She felt herself slipping into a strange sort of numbness. Her father was somewhere out there, so close, so close. He was hurt. He would probably be killed. And then it would be as she thought it had been already for so many years. But she would have lost him all over again.

"What else *would* he say?" Indigo's voice brought Rachel back to the place she was, in a strange clearing by a huge rock. He smiled at Rachel. "I told you he was good man. He doesn't want us to put ourselves at risk. But we will do what's right." He stood, slowly, as if his muscles were stiff. "You," he said to Malgam, "need to rest. As soon as we have some food and make a plan, you need to sleep."

"Do you have a plan?" Malgam looked grim.

Indigo smiled. "Not yet. But once we have some food in our bellies and we have all heard what you saw, we will. I'm going to fetch Pathik and Fisher, and we'll eat."

They built no fire; they were too close to the Roberts' camp to risk it. They made a dinner of dried meat and dried fruit. Malgam shared what he had seen.

"You said he was in a cage?" Pathik looked thoughtful. "What kind of cage?"

"Remember the book with the pictures of the old incarceration centers? Like that—the metal bars. But smaller, for some sort of animal, I think. And the back of it was solid, like they piled rocks against it." Malgam ripped a shred of dried meat from his piece and chewed while he thought. "The campfire was far off, but not so far we'd have much time to dig under, assuming that the cage doesn't have a bar floor under the dirt."

"First thing we'll need to do is kill the guard." Peter spoke quietly. Malgam scowled in Peter's general direction. Pathik just shook his head. Rachel made a *hmmph* sound before she could stop herself.

Indigo was the one who replied.

"We don't need to kill anyone, Peter, not unless they are trying to kill us."

"The Roberts would as soon kill you as look at you, from what you say about them." Peter spat the words. He turned from Indigo to Rachel. "They tortured your *father*. As far as you know they plan to kill him, or worse, trade him to the government. Doesn't that make you angry?"

Rachel nodded, her eyes wide. She *was* angry. She could feel it, a hot, hard place in the back of her throat. It had been there, really, for as long as she could remember.

"So we turn into them?" Indigo wasn't addressing Peter any longer. He was asking Rachel. "We decide that we can *kill* them because what they do is wrong?"

Rachel took her time, turning away from Peter to look at Indigo. She could not speak.

"You know the answer in your heart, Rachel. Or maybe it's in your head. I find it's usually a combination of the two that leads me best." Indigo smiled, that gentle, kind smile of his. Then he turned back to Peter.

"Let's hope nobody gets killed, Peter. Shall we?"

"We can use Rachel's cutter." Pathik jumped up and got his pack. He dug through it, removing a blanket and a pair of socks, and then the laser saw. "It worked on the sheet metal back at camp. I bet it will work on the cage bars. We'll need to knock the guard out." Pathik gave Peter a pointed look. "Then we can cut through some bars and get Daniel and go." Pathik bit his lip, thinking. "Best if we hit the camp as soon as it gets truly dark. That way they'll all be inside and we'll have less chance of being seen." He looked around to see if the others agreed.

"Here's Nipper." Nandy sounded relieved.

The Woolly bounded out of the forest and into the center of the group. He stood for a moment, assessing the state of things, and then sat elegantly next to Nandy. He looked at her, clearly awaiting her gratitude, and Nandy gladly gave it.

"*So* wonderful, Nipper. We thank you so much. And we are so sorry we ever said anything derogatory about your skills, aren't we, Malgam?" Nandy stroked Nipper's head. Malgam grumbled. Nipper growled.

"Based on how long it took him to get back here, we should be able to get an hour's rest, go get Daniel out, and head back to camp before the next dusk. While we're gone, you'll need

to keep watch and pack up. We'll want to be ready to move."
Malgam pointed at Rachel. "Maybe you can take first watch,
and then Indigo, since you two will be staying here."

"I'm going," said Rachel.

"You're too young for this, Rachel."

"Pathik's going. We must be around the same age."
Rachel spoke calmly. She wasn't going to let Malgam stop
her from going.

"You've no experience out here. You'll be more trouble
than good there."

"She did pretty well on the trek to camp from the Line."
Pathik wouldn't look at Rachel. "I mean, *just* okay." He
snuck a sidelong glance at her, a ghost of a grin touching his
mouth. "She did slow us down a day."

"I'm going—"

"She should go." Indigo decided it. "Daniel is her father.
Whatever happens, she should have the chance to be a part
of it. You, Malgam, are not going. You're too weak yet to
really be of help there. You and I will stay here. Peter, Pathik,
Rachel, Nandy, and Fisher will go."

"Heemmmmmm." Nipper made his sound, a cross
between a hum and a growl.

"Nipper's in." Nandy grinned. "Malgam, you should take
first watch if you're to be lazing about here." She ducked to
avoid the wadded-up cap Malgam threw at her.

Soon all who were not on watch were asleep. Even
Rachel, who felt so tense she couldn't imagine sleeping
when she lay down on her bedroll.

CHAPTER 10

PATHIK TOUCHED RACHEL'S cheek to wake her. She could barely see his face, floating ghostly pale, inches from hers. There was a heavy cloud cover, and the light from the moon was completely veiled. She rubbed at her eyes, and shook her head, trying to clear it. Pathik took her hand and led her through the murky dark to where the others stood together. As her eyes adjusted to the dark, Rachel could see that all were ready to go.

"Does everyone understand?" Indigo looked around the group. Everyone else nodded. Rachel wondered what they were all supposed to understand.

"But it won't go that way." Fisher spoke softly.

"If it does go that way, you need to be ready to leave whoever gets taken." Malgam sounded gruff. "That means any of you."

"What are you talking about?" Rachel didn't like the sound of it.

Malgam turned toward her. "If something goes wrong, Rachel, the most important thing is to get as many of you as possible out of that camp alive. That might mean leaving someone behind."

"Oh." Rachel thought about that.

"We'll be ready to move when you return. It won't take us long to break camp." Indigo nodded toward Malgam. "If there's anything we need to know, Nandy, you can show Malgam."

"No." Nandy looked at Malgam and even in the dark Rachel could see the love in her eyes. "You're too worn out from last night. Don't waste your strength waiting for me to show you anything. Either we come back fine or we don't. And I say we'll come back fine."

Malgam grinned at her. "You will, love. I know you will. But in case showing me something will help, you better show me. I'll be tempted to look anyway."

"Did you learn nothing from Usage? That's why there're rules in place, so those such as you have to behave." She singsonged her next words at him, shaking her finger in a mock scold. "No engagement without permission, unless a life's at stake."

"Perhaps now is one of those times when lives *are* at stake." Malgam reached out and grabbed her hand. He brought it to his lips and kissed it softly. "Come back to us."

Nandy smiled gently at him. "I will. We all will."

* * *

THEY WENT SINGLE file, with Pathik leading. Nandy and Rachel came next, then Peter, followed by Fisher. Nipper was somewhere off to their left, slipping silently through the trees. Rachel didn't like having Peter behind her. She touched Nandy's hand to let her know she was dropping back, and let Peter pass her.

"All well?" Fisher's voice was so low she barely heard it.

"Just more comfortable with friendly eyes at my back." Rachel adjusted the laser saw where it was tucked inside her jacket. Pathik had taken it from its case and handed it to her earlier.

"You'll be doing the cutting if it needs doing," he'd said with a grin.

They walked as quietly as they could. With no light it was slow going, and many times they all came to a complete halt while Pathik cut through branches with his knife or passed a warning down the line about a hole or a fallen tree. Peter held a bramble away for Rachel once, waiting for her to pass by it. Instead, she took hold of the branch and told him to go ahead. He started to speak, but Fisher shushed him. Finally he just shook his head and moved on.

The stench from the Roberts' camp intensified, filling the air, and once Rachel thought she might actually vomit. It was too dark to see well, and there were mounds of waste from the camp everywhere, it seemed. Rachel did her best to miss stepping in any of them. She wondered what kind of people would live like that. She had a bad feeling that she knew the answer.

After what seemed like forever, Pathik held up his hand. Nandy echoed the gesture, as did the rest down the line, until they all halted. Pathik dropped back and gathered them all together.

"It's just ahead," he whispered. "I came this far yesterday. There's a rough wall, low, that they built around camp. I don't know where the cage is—didn't go any closer than this."

"First thing we need to do is scout for sentries." Peter crouched down, gesturing for the others to join him. "The wall will be guarded." He pointed east. "I can check that way. Fisher, you can go west. Pathik can stay here with Nandy and Rachel. Once we've checked as far as we can and knocked out any we find, we come back here."

Pathik nodded. Fisher and Peter vanished into the dark. Nandy, Rachel, and Pathik waited, crouched silent in the chill. Rachel strained to hear any noise, any indication that either Fisher or Peter had found a guard. All she could hear was Nandy's soft breathing.

Then, a shuffle of leaves on the forest floor, a twig snapping, and Fisher appeared, breathless.

"One down," he panted. "He never even saw me. I hit him on the head and stuffed his mouth with my scarf. Tied his wrists too." Fisher looked around. "Where's Peter?"

As if in answer Peter returned, as breathless as Fisher had been.

"Nothing." He looked at Fisher. "Did you find one?" Fisher nodded. "Not too far."

"I went pretty far." Peter shook his head. "No way to

know if there was more than one on this side of the camp, but I'm betting not."

"We move in, then." Pathik rose. "I just wish we knew where the cage was."

"We do." Nandy pointed to the trees, where Nipper was emerging. "At least one of us does."

The Woolly slunk up to Nandy, rubbing against her knees briefly. Nandy leaned downed and scratched Nipper's forehead.

"Can you lead us, Nipper? Take us to Daniel?"

Nipper reared up and batted at Nandy's hair. He sat down and gazed up at her.

"Hrrrmmmmmmm." Nipper sounded troubled.

"I know." Nandy stroked Nipper some more. "But we have to get him out."

The Woolly growled low in his throat. He snuffled at Nandy, nudging her hand. Finally he sighed, as if he knew he wouldn't be able to change her mind. Then he leaped away, looking back once before moving slowly west toward the low wall.

The group followed.

The low wall was formed from what looked like mud bricks. They cleared it easily, after peeking over it to see what they could of the camp. There was little light, just the smoky embers from a large central fire pit. There were huts here, but they were nothing like the huts in Indigo's camp. These were tiny, sloppily built, and ill-kempt. Some looked deserted. There was no sign of a cage.

"Nipper?" Nandy whispered the Woolly's name.

Nipper strode back to her and rubbed her knees again. Then he walked away, toward the fire pit.

"Malgam said he saw the fire at a distance." Nandy stopped to think. "The cage must be on the other side of the fire pit, the other side of camp."

"Nipper may be able to walk right through their camp, but we stay low, next to the wall. We'll skirt the camp as best we can to get to the other side." Pathik began to move along the wall in the direction Nipper had gone.

They edged along, trying to stay as low and stealthy as possible. The wall began to curve away from them, and as they rounded the bend, the cage rose before them. There was no sign of any guard.

The cage was smaller than anything designed to hold a human, and divided into three cells. It looked like a picture Rachel had seen in a book—one of the old-fashioned, real books her mother liked so much—of a cage in a zoo. Like the zoo cage had been somehow set down in the middle of the clearing. Rachel wondered if there had been a zoo here once, long ago, long before the bombs and the Line and Away.

The back wall of the cage was built up on the outside with rocks, just as Malgam had seen. Each cell was completely exposed to the weather; there was no roof besides the bars, and no shelter within the cells. As they drew near, a break in the clouds allowed the moon to shine through, and Rachel could make out a crumpled shape on a dirt floor in the first cell. It looked like a pile of old rags. She approached with a sense of dread, which quickly became horror.

A skull gleamed in the pale moonlight. Its cheek rested on the perfectly preserved bones of a hand, in an oddly comfortable way, as though the former owner had curled up for a nap there. There was long, brown hair still attached to the skull. Rachel gasped when she saw it. For a moment she wondered if it belonged to her father. But the bones had been picked clean by some sort of scavenger long ago, and Malgam had seen through her father's eyes only yesterday.

"Nipper, old boy." A whisper, scarcely louder than a breeze.

Rachel saw Nipper at the third cell, poking his nose through the bars. A filthy, bloody hand reached out, trembling, and ruffled the fur on the Woolly's head.

Pathik motioned to Fisher and Peter to keep watch and scrambled to the cell. Rachel stayed where she was, suddenly frozen.

"Daniel?" Pathik barely breathed the words.

"Pathik." The voice sounded so weary.

"How do we open it?" Pathik ran his hand over the bars until he located a lock.

There was no reply for the longest moment. When it finally came, it was bereft of hope.

"You don't. I've tried every way." Daniel laughed softly, the sound colored with anguish. "They have a key somewhere for that lock, but who knows where. I told Malgam not to come."

Rachel saw his hand—her father's hand—take hold of Pathik's wrist.

"You need to go, Pathik. You and whoever else came, get

out of here as fast as you can. They have patrols out at night. If they find you . . . Just go."

His voice sounded so broken, nothing like the voice Rachel had so often imagined in her daydreams.

"We're not leaving you, Daniel." Nandy crept forward so Daniel could see her. "How bad are you hurt?"

"It doesn't matter. I can't get out of this cage, Nandy. The bars are steel—" Daniel fell silent and stared at the lowest corner of his cell, where a line of light traced its way across the bars. The light bloomed in the night.

"That's a laser saw!" Daniel forgot to whisper.

"Shhh." Pathik looked behind them, then turned back to Daniel. "Yes. We . . . we thought we might need it."

Daniel lowered his voice. "Where did you get a laser saw? Who's the girl?" Daniel lowered his voice even more, to a confidential whisper meant for Pathik alone. "Is she from the Roberts? They're . . . Pathik, they're doing some things with the government, things we hadn't even suspected."

Rachel looked up at that, and stared at her father. He was crouched in the cage, unable to stand. He looked back at her, the way a person looks at someone they don't know, and don't trust.

He didn't know her.

But then, why should he. She wouldn't have known him, not the way he looked now. She went back to work on the bars.

Pathik didn't waste time trying to explain. "Right now we just need to get you out of here, Daniel. We can talk later." He eyed Daniel's bloody hands, and the bruises mottling his face. "Can you walk?"

"I can *run,* if you can get me out of this cage." Daniel grinned, but he shook his head at the same moment. "I may need some help." He edged toward the bar Rachel was working on and grasped it below the top cut she had made. He grimaced as he closed his hand around it, pain from his injuries twisting his face.

"It might clang if it drops, once you finish that bottom cut." He met her eyes. "I'll hold it so it won't."

Rachel nodded, but she didn't speak. She didn't want her voice to betray the emotions she was feeling. She didn't even really know what they were. Daniel pulled the section of bar carefully away when she finished her cut and laid it on the ground.

Time surrounded Rachel, pressing at her, pushing in, making her hand shake when she tried to cut the next bar. She felt it like a change in the air pressure, the need to hurry, the urgency of the situation. She adjusted her grip on the laser saw and took a deep breath.

"You're doing great." Pathik was smiling at her when she looked at up. He reached out and touched a bar. "Just to here, don't you think?"

She looked; it was only one bar out from the one she was about to tackle. It did look like a man—especially a man as gaunt as Daniel appeared to be—could wriggle through the space three cut bars would make. She nodded at Pathik, and smiled as she realized he had given her the moment she needed to recover her composure. She applied the laser saw to the second bar with a steady hand. Time receded, leaving her to her work, and the world beyond the glow of the saw dimmed to a set of indistinct shapes.

When she made the last cut and her father laid the last section of bar in the dirt, it felt to Rachel as though there should be some sense of relief, but there was only fear. Her father was alive, his escape from horrible peril imminent, but he could be taken from her all over again, this time in front of her own eyes. She moved away from the opening in the bars and looked up at him.

"Come out," she whispered. "Come out now, and be careful. Be *careful.*"

Daniel gazed at her, puzzled. He didn't move. The strength of her emotion reached him; he felt it in all its heat. The cadence of her voice sang to him, like the memory of some other voice. He knew it; he knew it was . . . something.

He was tired. He was half starved. He'd been beaten daily for weeks. He didn't know the name of the song he was hearing. Still, it stunned him, and he crouched in his cell, motionless.

"Daniel." Pathik reached through the opening and took hold of Daniel's arm. "Time to go." He pulled. And Daniel blinked, released from his reverie. He shook himself, more a shudder than anything, and lowered his head to the opening of the cell. In seconds he had wriggled through to freedom.

Pathik took one arm and Rachel the other, and they supported him as he stood, for the first time since he had been locked in the cage. He stumbled; his legs were leaden and numb. They took small steps and he seemed to gain some strength. He cried out on the third step and grabbed his leg. Rachel could see blood seeping through his pant leg. But he straightened, determined, and went on. After they had covered a few feet he stopped them.

"The saw." Daniel looked at Rachel. "Get it out."

She had put it back inside her jacket. She reached for it, brow furrowed.

"Why?"

"It'll cut flesh as well as steel. We may need to cut some." Daniel whispered the words, but Rachel could hear the hatred in them.

Rachel shook her head and closed her jacket. She looked at her father's bloody hands and his bruised face. She wondered how many beatings it would take before she felt the kind of hate she heard in her father's voice.

"He's right." Peter appeared behind them. Fisher was with him. "Give it to me, Rachel, if you don't want to use it."

Daniel turned and stared.

"Peter?" He squeezed his eyes shut tight, then opened them again. He blinked rapidly. "Peter?" He turned to Rachel, a stunned expression on his face.

"Did he call you Rachel?" The words were faint, but Rachel could see her father looking at her as though he might know who she was, might remember her after all the long years, might see a three-year-old child in the girl standing before him. Might see his daughter.

"We have to get out of here," said Pathik. "Rachel, you and Nandy run and tell them we're coming. See if they can rig a pallet of some sort so we can carry him back to camp. We'll be right behind."

Rachel carefully transferred her father's arm to Peter, letting go only when she was sure he was firmly supporting Daniel. She shook her head at Pathik.

"You go ahead of us. We'll make sure nobody follows." With a pointed look at Peter she took the laser saw out from her jacket and held it tight, her finger on the activator button.

Pathik started to protest, but Nandy cut him off.

"She's right—they could pick you right off. Just start moving, and we'll watch the rear. We need to get out of here *now*." She dropped behind Rachel, taking out her knife and holding it low and close. Fisher joined her, unsheathing a similar weapon.

With Peter and Pathik in the lead supporting Daniel, they made slow, painful progress through the darkness. Rachel held the laser saw with both hands, and it still shook. She walked sideways, holding the weapon out toward the rear, scanning the blackness for any sign of someone following. Nandy and Fisher did the same.

They tried to be silent, but failed. Every footstep seemed to land on a branch, every breath rasped in Rachel's ears. Daniel cried out once, and they all froze in place. Six sets of ears strained to hear the sound of footsteps; six sets of eyes strained to see as far behind them as they could. After a long, tense interval, they set off again. The stench of the Roberts' camp hung heavy in the night air. They stopped occasionally, when Pathik raised a hand, to let Daniel rest. No one spoke.

Daniel did not cry out again, though his face twisted in pain. As they put more and more ground between them and the cage, Rachel felt her shoulders lower, and her breath came easier. She began to think maybe they would make it, maybe they would get back to the others safe. She looked at Fisher, and then at Nandy, trying to see their eyes in the gloom, to see if they felt the same sense of hope. She couldn't really tell.

Then she heard it.

It was fast, and worse, it was close. Pounding feet, hitting packed dirt, and the crackle of brush as men broke through it not far away. There were no shouted threats, no other sounds at all.

"Go!" Fisher gestured to Pathik and Peter. "Take Daniel and go. Hurry!"

Pathik hesitated. He looked at Rachel, torn.

"Pathik, please, get him out of here!" Rachel turned away as soon as she saw him start to move.

"Watch your side," whispered Nandy. She stood between Rachel and Fisher, her knife ready. Fisher reached into his jacket and pulled out a second knife. He held one knife in each hand, slightly out from his body, loose and ready. Rachel tightened her grip on the laser saw and braced herself.

The Roberts burst through the low bushes. There were two of them, and they had evidently expected to encounter backs, not faces. When they saw the three waiting, bristling with weapons, they came to a momentary halt. For a fleeting moment Rachel thought they would turn and run the other way. Instead, one leaped upon Nandy, pushing her to the ground. He had a club, and he raised it high above her. Fisher shot over to him and Rachel saw the flash of a knife blade, heard the man scream. His club fell and he grasped at his side. Rachel saw him rear back but then something hit her, hard, and she hit the ground.

The other man was on top of her, his fingers knotted through her hair. He smelled so strongly that Rachel felt nauseous. He had only one eye—the other was gone, an angry red scar in its place where someone had once done crude surgery.

He yanked her head up, exposing her neck, and when his other hand came into her field of vision she saw he had a knife. The blade glistened, slick with someone's blood. Rachel tried to flick the laser saw's switch, but he had her arm pinned to the ground. She could only watch as he brought the knife down.

There was a scream, and a blur of motion, and the man was swept off of Rachel. She scrambled to her feet, staring at a scene she didn't immediately comprehend. The man was writhing on the ground, something covering his face—something scratching and slicing and biting at his head. The man was screaming, and the sound mingled with the unholy shrieking coming from the thing on his head.

It was Nipper.

The man rose to his feet somehow, hands scrabbling at the Woolly, trying to pry the creature off of his face. Nipper hung on, hissing and spitting and inflicting more and more damage. He screamed shrilly when the man landed a blow.

Rachel was shaking all over. She looked down at her hand and saw that she still held the laser saw, her knuckles white from gripping it so tightly. She flicked the activator switch and watched as the thin beam shot forth from the handle. Another scream from Nipper rang out, and Rachel ran forward, slashing at the man's back with the laser. She saw his shirt split open, and his skin split just as fast. There was no blood, just a strange, red gash edged in white.

He ran then. He ran blind at first, with Nipper still riding his head. When Nipper leaped off into the bush he ran even faster. Rachel watched until she felt sure he wasn't coming back. Then she turned to see what had befallen her friends.

Fisher was helping Nandy up. She looked shaken, but she was uninjured as far as Rachel could tell. Fisher hadn't been so lucky; his right arm hung at his side and he winced as he pulled Nandy up with his left hand. Rachel saw some blood on his forearm.

"How bad is it?" Rachel reached for his sleeve.

"No time right now." Fisher scanned the night. "We need to go—they'll be gathering forces."

"Indigo is with us!" Nandy stood with her back to them, facing the dark forest. "Indigo is here!" she shouted again. She listened hard for a moment. Then she turned back to Rachel and Fisher.

Fisher looked at Nandy as though she had just burst into gibberish. "Shhhhhhhhhhhh," he said, holding his index finger in front of his lips in an exaggerated manner.

Nandy ignored him. "We need to stop the bleeding,

Fisher." Nandy produced a long strip of cloth. "Field dressings almost always come in handy." She nodded to Rachel. "Roll up his sleeve, Rachel."

"Are you crazy?" Fisher started to say more, but Nandy shushed him.

Rachel rolled back his sleeve, revealing a deep stab wound in Fisher's arm. Blood was oozing from it.

"At least he didn't hit any arteries." Nandy wrapped the wound tightly. "It's deep, though. And likely already infected. We'll need to see Saidon when we get back."

"If we get back." Fisher didn't sound afraid. He did sound worried. He kept looking in the direction the Roberts had run while Nandy finished wrapping his arm.

"They're gone," Rachel said as she rolled down his sleeve.

Fisher looked at her. "You were fierce. I think you may have saved Nipper's life."

"I think he saved mine." Rachel was suddenly aware of the pieces of bark in her hair, and the dirt she could feel on her face, and the fact that Fisher was staring at her.

Nipper materialized silently, limping. He stood, holding one of his front feet off the ground. Nandy started toward him but he moved away, in the direction of their temporary camp.

"He's right," said Fisher. "We need to keep moving."

"Let's go. I'll take a look at his foot once we're back home." Nandy strode after the Woolly. Fisher gestured for Rachel to go ahead of him, and they both followed Nandy's lead.

CHAPTER 11

THE CAMP WAS not packed up. The bedrolls were out and there was even a small fire. Fisher looked as confused as Rachel felt; they had been expecting to find the rest of the group ready to run for it as soon as they arrived.

"They'll be bringing more with them when they come back—shouldn't we be getting out of here?" Fisher took in the sight of grain mush warming over the fire with an incredulous look.

"Daniel needs rest before he tries to move." Indigo spoke quietly, though not quietly enough for Rachel's liking. She felt like the darkness was listening.

"Looks like you've been hurt too, Fisher." Indigo inspected the field dressing on Fisher's arm. "So we'll rest tonight, and head back home in the morning."

"They'll be coming, though." Fisher couldn't help repeating himself.

"They won't come until first light, I think. They might not come at all."

"What? Why would they wait until light to attack? They know we're here, they know they wounded one of us, they . . . they'll know we're having a nice meal soon enough, from the smell of the grain and the smoke from the fire." Fisher sounded flabbergasted.

"They also know Indigo is here. They won't come in the dark." Nandy exchanged a look with Indigo.

"Are you sure they heard?" Indigo sounded a bit worried.

"They heard. They were licking their wounds in the dark beyond the bushes until they heard me say your name. Then they ran away. I heard them go."

Indigo nodded. He took Fisher's arm in his hands and began to unwrap the field dressing. "Leave it for now," he said, when Fisher began to protest again. "I'll explain later." He turned to Rachel. "You should go to your father."

Her father. Rachel saw him, lying near the fire, with his head propped up by a bedroll. Pathik was cleaning his face, gently wiping away blood and dirt. Peter was cutting away Daniel's pant leg, in order to get a better look at a wound. Daniel was oblivious to all the activity—he was either asleep or unconscious.

"He's exhausted," said Pathik as she sat down next to him. "No killing wounds, so that's good. Saidon can help him heal when we get home." He shook his head. "They wanted him alive."

"He's just sleeping, right?" Rachel stared at Daniel's face, trying to find the smiling man from the digims her mother used to show her. She couldn't.

"Yes." Pathik brushed some dirt off of Rachel's sleeve. "Are you hurt anywhere?"

"I'm all right. A few scratches, but nothing else." The image of the Roberts man raising his knife above her flickered in her mind.

"They were going to trade him." Peter spoke, directing his words to Rachel. "He told us before he passed out, Rachel. They were going to trade him to the government."

Rachel looked at Pathik for confirmation.

"Yes." He nodded. "According to Daniel they have big plans. And he's not the first they've taken. But we'll talk about it later." Pathik tilted his head, eyes soft upon her. "You're sure you're all right?"

"I am."

"He knows you're his daughter." Peter spoke again. "He asked me before he passed . . . before he fell asleep. *It's Rachel, isn't it?* he said. I told him you and Vivian were fine."

Rachel shot Peter a look. She didn't feel fine. And for some reason she didn't like the idea that he had told her father anything about herself or her mother. She was about to say something to that effect when Indigo walked up to them. He held two wooden bowls of the grain mush, warm and fragrant. He handed one of them to Rachel. Nandy, Malgam, and Fisher followed with more bowls. Fisher still looked unhappy at the idea that they were staying. When those with extra bowls had passed them on, they settled down around Daniel to eat. He slept on, breathing steadily, obviously exhausted.

"Fisher." Indigo spoke quietly. "You asked why the Roberts won't come attack us in the dark. They won't come in the dark because it's a part of their superstition. They think everything evil is stronger in the dark. And they believe that I am evil."

"You? How would they even know of you? They haven't been near our camp in generations." Fisher looked skeptical.

"Three generations." Indigo's gaze took in his son, Malgam, and his grandson, Pathik, before he bowed his head. "They know of me because of something that happened many years ago, when I was just a boy. It was something I did—an accident." His next words were barely audible. "It was a horrible thing. It's the reason they haven't bothered our camp in so long."

Fisher looked at Nandy. "Is that why you shouted his name to the woods?"

Nandy was watching Indigo, her eyes shining with empathy for him. She nodded. "We knew it might be necessary to use their fear to keep them away from us. Especially if Daniel was hurt, as he is, and unable to travel quickly."

Fisher looked at the others, one at a time, before he spoke again. "It seems some of us here know more than others about the Roberts. Or at least about why the Roberts never bother our camp." He allowed his words to hang in the air.

"Some things aren't for your ears." Malgam sounded impatient, as usual.

"Ahh." Indigo raised a hand. "He should know. As should all of our people. Maybe they would understand the purpose of Usage better. Maybe they would understand why the council has always been so strict about our gifts, why *I've* always been so strict." He considered Fisher. "Your gift is to . . . well, I've always thought of your gift as a talent for asking the right question, or making the right observation, in just the right way." Indigo smiled. "As you just did when you said some of us knew more than others; you didn't press, or act outraged. You only observed, in a way that might inspire confidence sharing, as opposed to guilt or shame. You opened up an opportunity for me to tell you what you want to know, instead of making me feel like I should hide it from you."

Rachel frowned. "I thought you were good at catching fish."

The rest of them laughed, even Fisher.

"I am good at fishing. For information." He gave a modest shrug.

"I call it being nosy." Malgam was only half joking.

"It's a useful skill, regardless of what you call it, Malgam." Indigo chided gently with his tone. "But that's a discussion for another night. Tonight we need to talk about the Roberts, and about why they never bother our camp." He looked at the fire for a moment.

"Many years ago, when I was just a child, I discovered I

had a gift." Indigo shook his head slowly, almost imperceptibly. "If you can call my talent a gift."

Rachel and Fisher were the only two who seemed surprised.

"You were never named," said Fisher.

"No, I kept my birth name, Indigo. Given to me for the color of my eyes." Indigo smiled, but the smile faded quickly. "I never told anyone about my gift. So there was no naming ceremony for me, because nobody knew. And when a few did find out, they kept my gift from the rest of our people. For many reasons, all of them good. In the years that followed, I shared the nature of my gift with my family. But I have never told the rest of our people.

"I was about seven." Indigo returned his gaze to the fire, as though the flames held flickering images from that long-ago time. "I was sent for fire-starters—twigs and pinecones and the like. I wandered too far." He took a deep breath.

"There were three of them. Men from the Roberts camp. One of them grabbed me from behind, clamped his hand over my mouth. Another grabbed my legs and they carried me away from camp. When we were far enough away to risk stopping for a bit, they gagged me, so I couldn't make any noise, and tied my hands and feet. Then they dropped me on the ground as though I were already a corpse, tied me to a stump, and proceeded to have a snack. They talked about how they might use me to bargain for food stores from our camp, or whether it would be better to take me back to the Roberts camp as a slave."

Indigo looked at Pathik and Fisher. "You two don't remember a time when our camp was ever plagued by Roberts men. Neither do your parents." He glanced in Malgam's direction. "But there was a time. A time when they were many, and we were few, when we lived in fear of their attacks. They came at night to steal our women, or snatched our children from us in broad daylight. Those they took were never seen again, at least alive. Those who didn't hide their gifts were killed immediately; those without gifts, those who knew enough to hide them when they were caught, were taken as slaves. Often, their bodies were dumped on the edge of our camp when the Roberts were through with them, as a sort of warning. The bodies were always ruined; testaments to horrible suffering.

"That day, when they took me, I knew they were going to hurt me, maybe for a long time, and then kill me." Indigo paused. "I killed them instead."

There were gasps. Rachel looked around the campfire. Nandy, Malgam, and Pathik all had their heads bowed. It was clear they already knew the story. The gasps had come from Fisher and Peter. Fisher was staring at Indigo, his face a mask of shock. Peter was staring too, with something more like curiosity.

"That's your gift?" Fisher sounded horrified. "To kill?"

"As I said, I'm not certain it can be called a gift." Indigo raised his eyes to Fisher's. "I didn't know I could do it until I did. I was so afraid, lying there, listening to their plans for me. I was already farther from camp than I had ever been, and I thought I would never see my family again. I began to cry so hard that I almost choked—the gag in my mouth made it hard to breathe. One of them got up and walked over to me. I thought he might help me, remove the gag at least, but he just kicked me, hard, and told me to shut up. The other two laughed. And my fear kept building and building until . . . something happened.

"I could see a picture in my mind, a picture of a tube. And there was liquid flowing, pulsing, really, through the tube, and it scared me, because the fluid was blood. The blood of one of the men. I knew that, somehow. I also knew that if I could puncture that tube, I would be safe. So I tried, in my mind, to poke the tube, to make a hole in it and let all the liquid out. But I couldn't. All I could do was make the wall of the tube thinner, in one tiny place. So while the Roberts men laughed and ate, and I lay shivering in the dirt, I worked on that. It was hard. I scraped and scraped at that one place with my mind, until it got so thin it began to bulge, from the pressure of the blood flowing through. It got bigger and bigger, like a bubble. And finally, it burst, and all of the blood that was pulsing through the tube exploded outward."

Indigo had stopped seeing Fisher, or anyone else, while he told his story. He had gone to some inner vista, where that day he was captured was clear and vivid. Now his eyes refocused, and he was once again aware of the people around him.

"When that bubble burst, one of the Roberts men fell

where he sat. There wasn't a mark on him, but it was obvious he was dead. The other two were confused and afraid—they didn't know what had happened to their companion. But soon enough their eyes fell on me; they started toward me and I knew they were going to kill me." Indigo shook his head. "I killed one of them too, before I even really knew what I was doing. The third Roberts man ran—and when he reached his camp he told them about the killer boy with deep blue eyes.

"My father found me there just before nightfall, bound and gagged and sobbing, with two cooling bodies for company. He'd come looking as soon as the alarm was sent round that I was missing. I remember his face, one moment so filled with joy at the sight of me alive, the next filled with horror. I knew he understood, right away, that I had killed them."

There was silence. Nandy placed a hand on Indigo's shoulder.

"That's why the Roberts won't come here at night, why they may not come at all. It's why they haven't come near our camp for decades. They believe evil thrives at night; they believe I am evil.

"My father and the elders of our camp made sure the Roberts thought I could kill them all. They dragged the bodies of the Roberts men to the edge of their camp. They shouted to them. They told them the time had come for all of them to die; that the child was born who would do it, a child named Indigo. They told them their only hope was to leave us alone—that they might be spared if they kept away.

"They went further, even than that, to ensure our camp's safety.

"My father told me on his deathbed that the council at that time knew they had to take action against the Roberts. When I killed those men I gave the elders something they could use to frighten the Roberts. In order to leverage that fear, the council did something even more horrible than what I did. My killings were an accident; I had no way to know what I was doing. But the council men, my father included, snuck into the Roberts camp at night in twos and threes and killed people. They killed people who were sleeping, or who had stepped away from the safety of the main camp to relieve themselves. They strangled them, so that it might seem as though they died the same way the men who abducted me did. And then they drew blue eyes on the bodies, and left them to be found. They did this for weeks. They left the bodies as warnings. And it worked. The Roberts stayed away from our camp. At least they did, until lately. But what a stain on our history." Indigo looked sad.

"From your description, it sounds as though you were somehow able to cause aneurisms in those men, aneurisms that killed them almost instantly. No wonder the government wants to get their hands on subjects. I had no idea that your powers went that far." Peter looked fascinated.

"What do you mean by 'subjects'? And how do you know what the government wants? Unless you're working with them." Rachel glared at Peter.

"I'm on your side, Rachel."

"What about them? Are you on their side too?" Rachel gestured toward the Others.

Peter just shook his head.

"Enough of this," said Nandy. "Right now we all need to rest, if we can." She eyed Peter. "There will be time to uncover the truth about things when we're safe back at camp. I'm taking first watch." She looked worried.

"Nandy's right." Malgam stood. "We get as much rest as we can tonight and at first light we head for home."

Nandy strode to the edge of the firelight. She took out her knife and turned toward the darkness. The others settled into their bedrolls around the fire and tried to ignore the night sounds.

CHAPTER 12

Rachel."

The voice was her father's. So soft and gentle. Rachel opened her eyes. She could see the outlines of the nearest trees clearly; dawn was coming soon.

"Rachel."

It really *was* her father's voice—not a dream she had been having. Rachel sat up. He was awake too, a few feet away from her. She rummaged for a water container and brought it to him.

"Here. You should drink."

He looked at her for a long time before he took the water. Then he drank, deeply. She saw that he was crying. She didn't know what to say to him.

"I can't believe it's you." He whispered, so as not to wake the others.

"I feel . . . the same way. I—"

". . . thought you were dead." They spoke the same words

at the same time. Rachel smiled, and Daniel reached out his hand. She took it in both of hers.

"Well. Neither one of us is dead, Rachel. And I am so happy to see your face." He clasped his other hand over theirs, and squeezed. "I can see the three-year-old you in your features, believe it or not."

Rachel didn't say anything.

"I know." He nodded at her. "You probably don't remember me."

"I saw digims of you." Rachel wanted him to know he had been in her life.

"Only digims of me, and of a much younger me. I don't imagine I look anything like them right now." Daniel fell silent. He squeezed her hands again. "Rachel. Your mom. Is she really . . ."

"She's alive."

He bowed his head, his tears finally overcoming him. Rachel waited until he had wiped his eyes dry before she spoke again.

"She loved you, Dad. She still does. She never stopped hoping you were alive, all these years, even if she never said it out loud."

He nodded. "I thought you were both dead. All these years, I thought you were both dead."

"Dan." It was Peter. "Are you feeling like you can travel?"

"Peter." Daniel gave a half laugh. "I cannot believe this. You and Rachel, both here, both alive and well." Daniel frowned. "And Rachel tells me Vivian truly is alive and well. You told Indigo's man she was dead."

Peter looked confused. "What man?"

"There's a man in Bensen—Jard Thompson is what he goes by there. He's one of the Others. He's been there for many years—he was there before Indigo, even. He came to you soon after I was Called to Serve, didn't he? After they said I died?"

Peter nodded. "He did. He asked me about Viv, asked me if he could pay his respects for her loss. Everyone was under the impression you had died in the war, and that she was a widow. Even I didn't know for certain, though I had my suspicions that they had just used the Call to Serve as a way to get rid of you. He's one of them?" Peter looked astounded. "I thought he worked with you at the firm, or something like that."

"Why did you tell him Vivian and Rachel were dead?"

"I didn't. I told him exactly what I knew, which was that the apartment was empty and I couldn't find them."

Peter looked at Rachel when she snorted. "I tried to find your mom and you, Rachel. But the place where you lived was abandoned. I couldn't find any sign of you, or find out where you'd gone. I actually did think you were dead—I thought they came and took you. But that wasn't what I told Thompson—I only said I didn't know where you were."

"I don't believe you!" Rachel sneered at Peter. She turned to Daniel. "He said he'd bring us a key, and he brought the EOs instead."

"There's a misunderstanding, Daniel." Peter was calm.

"Rachel." Daniel reached out and took her hand. "Peter has been a friend of mine for many, many years. Let's hear what he has to say."

Rachel wasn't happy, but she grudgingly agreed.

"I still don't know exactly what Viv was up to, Danny." Peter smiled faintly. "She showed up out of the blue, after all those years—showed up on my doorstep asking for a key. It was right after they Identified Jolie and Trina—"

"They what?" Daniel looked horrified. "Oh Peter. I'm so sorry." He frowned. "But who is Trina?"

"Trina was . . . is our daughter. She was born after you got the Call to Serve," said Peter. "I still hope to see them again. I plan to use the maps, Daniel. I'm going to try to negotiate a trade."

"I don't have them, Peter. I left them with Viv when I went to Serve."

"I have them," said Rachel. She answered Daniel's surprised look. "Mom put some things in my pack."

Peter nodded. "She told me you had them that night when the EOs showed up at Ms. Moore's. That's why I Crossed. I hoped to find you and get you back to your mom, and also get the maps. I think they'll work a deal with me if I have the maps."

"So you really brought her a key?" Rachel was still skeptical.

"I really did."

"But you used a key to Cross."

"I did."

Rachel's lower lip was trembling. She did her best to sound brave. "So we can't get back."

"Well, that's the thing . . ." Peter stopped speaking. Both he and Daniel stared at the tree line.

"What's that?" Rachel whispered. Something was growling, low and loud.

"Where's the laser saw?" Peter didn't take his eyes off the trees.

"It's here." Rachel felt for the saw—she had tucked it in her bedroll before she slept. She found it almost immediately and held it up. Peter grabbed it.

"Try to get close to the fire. They're afraid of fire. Move very slowly." Malgam spoke in a hushed voice. He too had heard the growl.

Rachel looked over and saw that everyone else was awake, all eyes glued to the tree line. Nipper appeared from nowhere and crouched in front of Nandy, a snarl coming from his throat.

"What *is* it?" Peter's finger hovered on the laser saw switch.

"It's a baern." Malgam sounded grim. "It's hunting."

"I guess it eats people?" Peter didn't sound happy.

"Yes," Malgam whispered. "It eats people." He stared at the tree line. "You and Daniel and Rachel are the closest to it. You need to move first. Get around to the other side of the fire as quietly as you can. Don't move fast."

"Peter, take Rachel. I can't move well enough to get out of its way." Daniel didn't look at Rachel.

"I'm not going. Not without you." Rachel stared at her father, tears stinging her eyes. "I'm not losing you again."

"Rachel, now's not the—"

There was roar and a flash of movement. Rachel got only an impression: of muscled legs and yellowed teeth, of something huge coming down from above. She heard a scream, and wasn't sure if it was coming from her own mouth or from someone else. But then she heard it again, and she knew it was Peter. The baern had landed on him, knocking him flat on the ground. There was a flash of light in the predawn dimness, and another terrible scream, one that didn't come from human lips. The baern writhed and screamed again, then moaned, and collapsed on Peter. It quivered and then was still.

Only Peter's head and shoulders were visible. Rachel ran to him. He was still breathing. He opened his eyes and stared at her face, but she wasn't certain he saw her. He coughed, a weak, strangled cough, and scarlet spilled from his lips.

Pathik and Malgam were seconds behind Rachel. They shoved the baern off of Peter. He'd struck the thing's heart with the laser saw beam. But not before it managed, with a single claw, to slice him open from neck to navel.

Rachel felt cold. There was so much blood. Peter was gasping and reaching toward her.

"Rachel. Two . . . keys. In my pack. Two." He smiled weakly. "I always planned to give your mother one."

Rachel took the hand that kept reaching for her, and

gripped it hard despite the blood that covered it. Peter seemed to feel it, to know she was holding his hand. "You tell Daniel to get my girls. Tell him to get Jolie and Trina back. Like I would have for him." He whispered the last words. And then he died.

CHAPTER 13

THEY HAD TO leave the body. They made their way back to camp somehow, but Rachel didn't remember much of the trip. She knew Pathik was near her, and her father was there too, though he was weak. She remembered stumbling through the bush, tripping and almost falling, feeling cold and numb at the same time. She remembered Peter's bloody eyes. She wanted to go home.

A sentry must have seen their approach and alerted the camp, for there was a quiet group waiting for them when they arrived. Michael was there, and Saidon, the healer, along with several others Rachel didn't recognize.

"Saidon is ready for Daniel. There's a room set up for him." Michael eyed Fisher's arm. "Looks like you should go with them. The rest of us need to gather and talk. I've had the council room set up with hot root brew and food."

"I'm fine," said Fisher. "I'll join the meeting."

"Maybe you could give me a hand with Daniel first."

Pathik looked amused at Fisher's eagerness to be included in the council meeting.

"I'd be pleased to, Pathik." Fisher didn't sound pleased, but he was quick to help. He and Pathik each took one of Daniel's arms and started toward the hospital. Rachel and Saidon followed.

"Rachel." Indigo's voice drew her back. "I know you want to be with your father, but I think you should come to the council meeting first."

Rachel hesitated.

"I'll take good care of him." Saidon smiled at Rachel. She exuded calm assurance. Rachel nodded.

"I'll be with you soon, Father." She wasn't sure if Daniel heard her; he seemed to be on the edge of consciousness. The trek back to camp had taken all his energy.

The council room was equipped with bowls of steaming water, scented with some astringent oil, so the weary band could refresh themselves. There was, as Michael had said, hot root brew and an assortment of food. Rachel soaked a rough cloth in one of the bowls of fragrant water and wrung it out. She couldn't remember a better feeling than the warm, clean cloth against her neck. She washed as much grime off of her face and hands as she could. Then she helped herself to some food—there was bread and dried meat and some dried berries. With a brimming plate and a cup of root brew, she found a place to sit on one of the benches.

Once they had all settled, Michael, who had been waiting at the front of the room, addressed them.

"Where is Peter?"

"He's dead." Indigo sounded as drained as Rachel felt. "Killed by a baern. But we can discuss that later. Right now, we need to make some decisions.

"We have good reason to believe that our greatest fears are true. The Roberts were planning to trade Daniel to the government. From what he says, they've traded two others already." Indigo paused, to ensure all had heard him. "Two others," he repeated. "Who do you think they might be?"

There was a cry from behind Rachel. She turned, shocked at the sound of it—it sounded so full of anguish. A woman sat two rows back, her head bowed, her hands covering her face. Another woman quickly led her out of the room.

"Are you suggesting that the Roberts took Ivy's sons— that they were traded?" Michael looked shocked. "Did Daniel see them with his own eyes?"

"No. He heard the Roberts talking," said Indigo.

"That's no proof. For all we know the boys were taken by a baern as we suspected."

"It's proof enough for me. The Roberts plan to take those they can and trade us for goods. And they don't care what happens to us in the government labs." Indigo addressed the rest of the room. "I won't have us tested and tortured and used for ill. I won't have our gifts turned into evil. We have a chance on Salishan. We need to take it."

"How are we any better off if we uproot our people from the safety of this camp, risk their lives in a water crossing where the boats are probably ruined *if* they even exist anymore, and take them to a place we know nothing about except what's spun in old men's firetales? For all you know the bombs rendered it sterile."

"They didn't render our land sterile. At least not permanently." Indigo's eyes flashed. Rachel had never seen him look so angry. "Let's ask, shall we? Since we have someone here who might actually know what became of Salishan after the bombing."

Rachel waited, wondering where Salishan was, and who would know whether it was sterile. It took a moment for her to realize that Indigo, and all the others in the room, were looking at her.

"What?"

"Do you know, Rachel? Is Salishan sterile? After they evacuated, did they track what happened to the island?"

"What island? Is Salishan an island?" Rachel thought; she didn't remember any island called that.

"It was evacuated before Unifolle's Border Defense System was activated. They built their system before the Unified States did, so they had time to plan things better," said Indigo.

"Maybe it's called something else now." Nandy spoke up. "Salishan is how it's listed in our records, but that name is just what the survivors of the bombs called it." Nandy looked at Rachel. "Our forebears wrote down everything they could think of, in case we might need the knowledge someday. We have preserved their writings as much as we could. They wrote about what the world was like before they were trapped here, at least what they knew. They tried to record whatever they thought was important, everything from the history leading up to the decision to abandon people here, to how to smoke fish in order to preserve it."

Rachel nodded. "I think they must have been talking about the relinquished islands. There were a couple of them. One very large, a couple of smaller ones. They were left out of Unifolle's border plans because the expense to include them would have been exorbitant. They did evacuate people from them and relocate them on the mainland."

"The large one—is it sterile?" Indigo sounded impatient.

"I don't know," said Rachel. "It's never really talked about. It's not like people are allowed to go there."

Michael gave Indigo a pointed look.

"Means nothing," said Indigo, though he sounded disappointed that Rachel didn't know. He turned away from Michael. "Rachel, thank you. I think you should go tend to your father now. We have things to settle here."

WHEN RACHEL KNOCKED on the battered metal door of the hospital it was opened by the same wavy-haired man who had opened it before. He stepped back when he saw her, and the look on his face was a mixture of fear and distaste. In that moment, Rachel realized that *she* was the reason he had rushed away so quickly the last time she was here. She had thought it was Malgam who frightened him.

"Here for your da, I suppose."

"Yes." Rachel frowned at him. He didn't even know her, yet he acted as though she was a bad person.

"He's in the same room Malgam was. So you know the way." The man made no offer to escort her down the dim corridor.

"Is there a light I can use?" Rachel wasn't sure she did know the way. She remembered that there had been several doors off the corridor. She remembered it had been dark.

The man grunted. Grudgingly, he retrieved one of several oil jars perched on a shelf and lit its wick. He handed it to her.

"Thanks." She hesitated only a second before her pride propelled her toward the corridor.

It was as dark as she remembered, but she found her way. She passed several closed doors before she came to the room in which she thought Malgam had convalesced. There was light underneath that door. She knocked quietly, and immediately heard footsteps.

"Rachel?" It was Pathik's voice, low but audible from the other side of the door.

"Yes."

The door opened. Beyond Pathik, Rachel could see her father lying on the same metal bed Malgam had been in, his face unnaturally pale, glistening with sweat. The healer, Saidon, was seated in a chair next to his bed, her hands on his injured leg. Her eyes were closed and Rachel saw, as she drew nearer, that she was trembling.

Pathik led her nearer. She knew, somehow, with no words exchanged, that now was not the time to speak. So she stood, and let Pathik hold her hand, and watched. Daniel smiled at her when he saw her, but he remained silent.

Saidon breathed deep and even, and she pressed her hands gently on Daniel's leg with each inhalation. Rachel could see the wound clearly, and it looked much worse than she had thought it was during their trek back to camp. She didn't understand how he had managed to walk on that leg at all.

For a time there was no sound other than that of Saidon's breathing. The wound didn't change in appearance at all, though Rachel had half expected to see it mend before her eyes. But Daniel's face did get more relaxed. He looked as though his pain was easing as Saidon worked on his leg. She took a few more measured breaths and then opened her eyes. She took her hands off Daniel's leg, and rubbed them together as though they were stiff. When she looked at Rachel it was as though she was looking from someplace very far away.

"He'll need time to recover. His leg is infected. He has many other wounds, too, though none so severe." Saidon shook her head. "They are savages."

"Saidon." Pathik spoke softly, but there was a note of admonishment in his tone.

"I know, Pathik, I know your grandfather would like us to hold our judgment. And I do, most times. But when I see something like these wounds—these wounds are meant to torture, Pathik. Those Roberts knew exactly what they were doing to him. And they probably enjoyed it." Saidon started to say more, but she bit her lip. She looked tired. "I'll go now. But I'll be back tomorrow for another session. It will take a few more." She put a hand on Rachel's shoulder. "He's lucky, and he's strong. As long as he can rest and eat he should be fine."

"Thank you," said Rachel. She wasn't certain exactly what she was thanking the healer for, but she knew her father looked less strained than he had when she'd arrived.

Saidon smiled. "You're welcome, child. Your father has always been good to me. To all of us here." She turned to Pathik. "Can you walk me out, please? I imagine these two have some talking to do."

"I'll come back in a little while," said Pathik. Rachel nodded. When the door closed behind them, she went to her father.

He was still awake, though he must be exhausted. Rachel sat in the chair Saidon had used. She watched his face, her father's face. For a time, he simply watched her too. Then he smiled again.

"I see your mother in you."

Rachel smiled back at him. "She always says I look like you."

"Maybe a bit. But I see her beauty in your face." His smile slipped away. "I missed so much."

Rachel said nothing. She thought of her mother, and wondered if she was fixing a meal for Ms. Moore, or getting ready to go to Bensen for supplies. She imagined walking into the parlor of Ms. Moore's house with Daniel, and watching Vivian's face light up with joy.

"We have to get Mom." She realized just after the fact that she'd spoken aloud.

Daniel nodded. "We will." He looked at his leg and sighed.

"You do have to rest first, Dad. But as soon as you can, we have to get her."

"I notice you're not saying get *back* to her," said Daniel. He looked very serious. And something else—he looked proud.

"We can't stay there. Can we?" Rachel already knew the answer. "We'll have to come back here."

"We'll come back here for a short time," said Daniel. "But we'll go to a different place. I think we might be safe there." He sounded as tired as he looked.

"You mean Salishan?"

Daniel started. "What do you know about Salishan?"

"Nothing. They were talking about it in the council meeting. Indigo wants them to go there. That man called Michael doesn't."

"Indigo's right. We have a chance, I think, if we go there. It's a huge island, from what Indigo's notes say. We might be able to live there, without worrying about the Roberts *or* the government." Daniel frowned. "Do you really have the maps, Rachel?"

"Mom put them in my pack. She wrote me a letter too,

and explained that they were important, but she didn't say why. Just that I'm supposed to be very careful with them and not let anyone get them." Rachel looked behind her at the door. It was firmly shut. She lowered her voice to a whisper. "What are the maps, Dad? And why don't they look like maps?"

Daniel hesitated. "Only a very few of us should know." He waited until Rachel nodded. Then he continued, his voice as hushed as hers had been. "People from the collaboration risked their lives—some lost their lives—to get the information that is on those papers. They may not look like maps, but they are—maps of borders.

"They're schematics, really, showing the details of various border defense systems. The U.S. is there, along with some of the countries the U.S. would like to invade. The schematics include the weaknesses. These weaknesses aren't much use to anyone by themselves—every system has some weaknesses, but they aren't the kind that would allow a country to get troops inside enemy territory. However, they are the kind that would allow one or two people to slip through a system. And the U.S. wants to be able to do that very much."

Rachel frowned. "What good would it do the U.S. to get one or two people through another country's defense system? They couldn't take over that way. They would just get shot or locked up or something, wouldn't they?"

"You're right, Rachel. If they were Regs, they would be shot or locked up. But the U.S. doesn't plan to send Regs." Daniel sounded angry.

Rachel didn't understand at first. But then it all clicked into place in her mind.

"You're saying they would send Others? Try to use them somehow because of their gifts?"

Daniel nodded. "They don't know exactly *what* the Others can do, but they know they can do something. I remember hearing from other collaborators about people in lab cages, being tested for things. None of us were sure what they were doing—we thought they might be torturing collaborators. Now I think it was some of the survivors. Indigo told me that there have always been stories of children disappearing here—when they started seeing children born with gifts, several vanished, according to the notes the early survivors left. They thought the Roberts took them, because it was soon after the split between them and the people here. But now I think that they were stolen by the government. I think they're still doing it too."

"Is that what they were talking about at the meeting?" Rachel felt sick. "They said two young boys were taken. Michael said they were killed by a baern, but Indigo sounded like he didn't think so."

"I don't think so either. I think they're in a government lab somewhere right now."

"But the Others wouldn't help the U.S., would they? The U.S. left them on the other side of the Line, abandoned them to whatever might happen. They didn't care if the bombs fried every last one of those people all those years ago. Why would the Others help them?"

"Well—"

"And besides! What good would it do? I mean, all the Others can do is move packs a couple of inches or feel if people are lying or . . . see what other people see." Rachel's eyes grew wide. "Or kill people."

Daniel took her hand. "I believe the U.S. thinks they could take over a government, and then a country, if they managed to place just a few key players in the right spots. With the right gifts, used the right way, they might be able to do just that."

"But still, Dad, why would the Others help the U.S.? Even if they were told they would be killed if they didn't cooperate, why would they help them? The Others don't think much of Regs."

Daniel looked at Rachel. He squeezed her hand.

"There are worse things than dying. What would you do to protect your mom, Rachel, if somebody threatened her?" He let the question go unanswered.

Rachel thought of something. "Why did the collaborators copy the maps—what good would it do them? Did they want to sneak into other countries?"

"We copied everything we could get our hands on." Daniel grinned. "Any information the general public wasn't supposed to have, we wanted. I don't think they had a real plan for the maps, but I'm not really sure—we got all of our information passed down in bits and pieces. All I really knew was that I was supposed to keep them safe. The only reason I knew what they were was because Peter and I were both architects, so we were able to make some sense of the sets of numbers on them.

"The thing is, if we can get word to the government somehow that we have them, we might be able to bluff our way to them leaving us alone. They still don't know exactly what the Others are capable of doing."

"So they would be afraid to bother us?" Rachel liked that plan.

"Exactly."

"Dad." Rachel knew he needed to rest, but she had to ask. "Do *we*?"

"Do we what?" Daniel sounded so tired.

"Do we know what the Others are capable of?"

Daniel didn't answer. He'd finally drifted off to sleep.

CHAPTER 14

THE DAYS PASSED. Rachel wished they were already on their way to The Property. Still, she made certain she helped as much as she could at camp; she gathered more firewood than Pathik did, and setting up the classroom with Nandy was a regular morning chore.

"Can Rachel help teach class today?" Bender tugged at Nandy's shirt.

Rachel hid her grin and continued to distribute the sharpened sticks the children used to write in the sand trays.

"I thought you didn't like Rachel, Bender?" Nandy smiled at Bender while she scratched Nipper, who was, as always, reclining on one of the benches. His leg had healed well, and he seemed fit as he had ever been.

The boy's cheeks flushed with shame. "I was being ignorant." He looked up from beneath his lashes to see if using one of the previous day's vocabulary words was going to get him anywhere.

Nandy laughed. "Yes, Bender, you were being ignorant. It appears you've changed your opinion now. But I think Rachel wanted to observe Usage, so you and the rest of the gifted are going there today instead. The rest of us will work on math, and we'll do spelling tomorrow."

"But I practiced my words just so she could see! Can't you go to Usage tomorrow, when we usually have it, Rachel?" Bender used his most persuasive pout.

"I think we have plans for tomorrow, Bender." Rachel saw Nandy's questioning look and nodded slightly.

"Off with you now, Bender, and get the others." Nandy shooed the boy out of the room. She turned back to Rachel. "So it's tomorrow?"

"I think so. Dad's been feeling strong enough for a few days now."

Daniel had been resting and regaining his strength. His leg was almost completely healed, and he said he felt strong enough to make the trip back to The Property. The plan was to use one of Peter's key to Cross, find out if his wife and child were still alive, get them if possible. Then return, using the second key, with Vivian and Ms. Moore too, of course, and get to Salishan.

Rachel had asked about the keys during one of the evenings she spent with Daniel in his bakery building room—she wanted to know how Peter had come to have three.

"Military issue," Daniel had said. "When the Border Defense System was first activated, soldiers still Crossed fairly often for one reason or another, mostly diplomatic excursions to neighboring countries. Not along the Line, of course, but on other parts of the System. The keys were originally issued in sets of three to commanding officers who were going to Cross troops to escort diplomats. One for the trip over, one for the trip back, and one for insurance. Ideally, they were supposed to turn in two expended keys and one unused one at the end of a mission. Or have a convincing reason why they had to use the third. The collaborators got hold of some sets early on when one of the supply officers defected. The set Peter was in charge of safekeeping had been passed through the years from collaborator to collaborator."

"If you're going tomorrow I'm sure there'll be a council meeting tonight." Nandy's voice brought Rachel back to the schoolroom. "Michael will want to get his opinion registered, as he does about everything."

Rachel nodded. "I don't think it'll have much effect on Dad's plans. He has his mind made up that tomorrow is the day."

Nandy nodded. "I think Indigo agrees. He said he was going."

Rachel wasn't really surprised. She could see it in Indigo's eyes, hear it in the questions he asked her about The Property. He wanted to see Ms. Moore. She wondered what had been in Ms. Moore's letter to him.

"Well, off to Usage with you, young lady." Nandy smiled. She reminded Rachel of her mother just then.

Usage was held in the smaller of the two buildings next

to the hospital. Or at least the parts of Usage that could be held in such a small, interior space. Rachel had learned that it consisted of two parts: theory and practice. Theory was all about how gifts should be used, and it was held inside. Practice was just that—practicing gifts, honing them. Some practice was held inside, but some practice had to be held outside, depending on the gift.

Rachel paused at the door of the building. She was about to knock on it when it opened, and Pathik smiled at her from inside.

"Are you ready to observe?" He made a sweeping gesture with his hand, bowing and bidding her to enter the building.

"Oh, fancy," she said.

"Welcome, Rachel!"

Pathik's grin disappeared as Fisher came up behind him.

"I think we're all ready for you." Fisher smiled and reached over Pathik's head to hold the door open. "Let's go find you a place to sit."

Rachel started to enter but Pathik stepped in front of her. He turned to Fisher.

"We'll be in shortly."

Fisher continued to hold the door open, his arm over Pathik's head.

"Any particular problem?" Fisher tilted his head at Pathik.

"No problem at all, Fisher." Pathik smiled, a warning in the curve of his lips. "We'll be right there."

Fisher removed his hand from the door and let it fall toward Pathik, who stopped it with a foot. After a glance at Rachel, Fisher nodded.

"See you inside." He turned and left.

Rachel poked Pathik in the back, hard. "What?"

He turned to face her. "What?"

Rachel crossed her arms. " 'We'll be in shortly'?" She waited. "Did you have something you needed to talk with me about?"

"No." Pathik wouldn't meet her eyes. He scuffed the bottom of the door with his toe.

"Then, shall we go inside?"

Pathik opened his mouth to speak, but didn't. Finally he moved aside. "After you."

There were about a dozen kids in the room—some close to Rachel's age, but not all—sitting on the floor. She saw Jab, and Kinec. She recognized some of the others from having seen them around the camp. Indigo was at the front of the room and he smiled as Rachel came in.

"Welcome, Rachel. Have a seat anywhere."

Rachel chose a seat toward the back of the room. The whispers she heard as she settled in didn't sound exactly friendly to her. Pathik sat down next to her.

"Can we all welcome Rachel, please?" Indigo looked intently around the room.

"We agreed she could be here. Doesn't mean we're happy about it. A Reg, at Usage." Jab sounded disgusted. He didn't look at Rachel.

"Enough out of you, Jab." Pathik half rose.

"Enough out of both of you for now." Indigo motioned to Pathik to sit down.

"She might be a Reg, but she's a good one."

Rachel had to crane her neck to see the source of the comment. Bender, sitting near the front of the room, almost hidden since he was shorter than the rest of them. He grinned in her direction and she smiled.

"She brought medicine." Bender shook his finger at Jab. "She didn't have to do that."

"All right, all right, Bender." Jab didn't look convinced.

"We'll start today with a brief explanation for our guest," said Indigo. "Rachel, you know some of us have gifts."

Rachel nodded.

"Usage is our practice of those gifts, and our study of how we use them." He waited to see if she had any questions. Rachel kept silent.

Indigo addressed the whole room. "Today, let's focus on control. We'll save experimentation for next time." Indigo nodded toward Bender. "Bender, would you like to show us your progress?"

Bender leaped up; he was an eager student here, unlike in school. He walked to the front of the room and stood next to Indigo. From his pocket, he extracted a metal rod. It was about six inches long and about an inch in diameter. Rachel wondered what it had come from; one end was twisted and jagged where it had been broken from something.

Bender held it at eye level in front of him. He stared at it. After a minute or so the rod bent, so that it formed an upside-down L. Bender tilted his head a bit and the L became an upside-down V.

"Very good!" Indigo patted Bender's shoulder. "And back?"

Bender tapped at the bend in the metal. "Still too hot." He blew on the rod, cooling it. After a few more minutes he stared at it again. The V became an L, and then the rod straightened back to the way it was at the beginning of the exercise.

"You make that look so easy!" Kinec was grinning at Bender from the floor.

"But I can only do metal, Kinec," said Bender, looking proud despite himself at the older boy's praise. "You can do anything."

"That was very much improved, Bender, over last session." Indigo looked pleased. "You have been practicing well."

"Thanks." Bender's cheeks turned rosy. "I worked on it every night."

"Who's next?" Indigo looked around. A girl, younger than Rachel by a year or two, raised her hand. Indigo beckoned to her.

"Serena."

The girl rose and took Bender's place. Indigo looked at the students again. "A volunteer?"

"I will." Fisher spoke, but he remained where he was.

Indigo nodded. "Whenever you're ready," he said to Serena. She nodded, and smiled shyly at Fisher. She took a deep breath, and brushed at her hair with one hand.

"Is it deep trouble, or light?" She watched Fisher carefully.

"I'd say it's somewhere in between," said Fisher. He looked pointedly at Rachel. Returning his gaze to Serena, he continued. "I'm unable to sleep well, at times. And I feel a certain melancholy."

The girl nodded. She closed her eyes, and her hand crept up toward her hair again. She pressed two fingers to her temple, and the other fingers splayed out away from her brow.

The room was silent. Rachel noticed that nobody watched the girl; they were all looking at Fisher. She looked too. At first, she didn't notice anything. But then, there was a shift, something so subtle it happened almost invisibly. Fisher's face relaxed, just around the eyes. That was all. Rachel looked at Serena and saw that she was smiling softly, her eyes still closed. Fisher didn't smile, but he looked the way someone does when some pain, a headache, a sore muscle—inconsequential but wearying—eases.

Indigo placed his hand on Serena's shoulder and she opened her eyes.

"I could feel it a lot better this time—I knew right when it was soothed for him." Serena looked excited.

Indigo nodded. "It seemed like it was easier for you to

get there this time." He looked toward Fisher. "How do you feel?"

Fisher allowed himself a smile then. "Just like she said. Soothed."

"Excellent work, Serena." Indigo waited while the girl sat down.

"Now. I know we haven't all practiced yet, but I want to move on to our study. That way Rachel will be able to have a general sense of all that we do in Usage class before she leaves us. Do you have any questions, Rachel, before study?"

Rachel hadn't realized she wasn't staying for the entire Usage class. She tried to hide her surprise. "So, gifts come in different strengths? Or are they harder for some than others?" Rachel remembered the beads of sweat on Kinec's forehead when he had made his pack move during the trek to camp. Bender's face had betrayed no great effort when he bent his steel rod. She didn't remember that Jab had looked particularly strained when he hurt her either.

"We don't know all the answers about our gifts, Rachel. They do come to us with varying degrees of power. But practice does seem to make a difference."

"And how do you decide whether you *should* get better, at a gift?"

Indigo nodded. He knew Rachel was thinking of his kind of gift. "That's a hard question to answer, Rachel. I do believe some gifts should not be honed."

"What sort of gift should not be used, if it's given?" Jab sounded defensive, as if he knew the answer.

Indigo spoke quietly. "Just because a person can do something, does it always mean they should?"

Jab didn't answer.

"I'd like to have a talk with you, Jab, after Usage." Indigo looked at Rachel for a moment, then addressed the room again. "But let's talk about this a little now." He pointed to Bender. "When, Bender, would it be wrong for you to use your gift?"

Bender spoke by rote. "If I trespass on another unbidden."

Indigo smiled. "Precisely. But what does that mean, Bender?"

Bender shrugged.

"If I asked you to help me by straightening my knife, could you use your gift?"

Bender nodded. "But if you didn't ask, and I just did it, it would still be helping you."

Indigo nodded. "If Serena used her gift without asking you, would it be helping?"

Bender thought. "I don't see why it wouldn't. She makes people feel better."

"I make people feel less." Serena spoke. "That's my gift, Bender. I take away feeling. Not permanently. But that's what I do. And sometimes, if a feeling isn't good, it helps someone to feel better." She looked at Indigo for permission to continue. He nodded. "When I get really good at my gift, I'll be able to make you feel nothing at all if I want to, Bender. Would you want me to do that?"

Bender frowned. "I don't think so."

"So that's why we have study. Why we have to think about

when it's right to use our gifts, how we can use them wisely."

"At least you'll be able to, though." Jab scowled at Serena. "You have a gift you *can* use. Some of us have bad gifts. Or so some say." He glowered at Indigo.

"There is no such thing as a bad gift." Indigo spoke firmly. "There are only bad ways to use gifts." Indigo looked around slowly, making certain every person heard his words. "I think we can end early today. I thank you all for allowing Rachel to observe." People began to file out of the room. "Jab." Indigo motioned to the boy to come to him. "You and I need to have a discussion."

Rachel saw them later, sitting on two stumps at the edge of the camp. Jab was listening intently to Indigo. She wondered if Indigo was telling him about his own gift. Rachel wondered if Indigo was telling Jab how he might use his gift in good ways. She couldn't think of any.

THE COUNCIL MEETING was short. Michael was there, as was most of the rest of the camp. Word had gotten out that there was a trek planned. And somehow, it seemed common knowledge that the trek was to the Line, back to the place Indigo had gone so many years ago, the place where he had fallen in love with a Reg, and fathered her son. People were chattering in gossipy, low tones. Pathik and Indigo arrived a bit late. Indigo strode once again to the front of the room.

"Daniel has recuperated well from his injuries." The crowd quieted. "The Roberts have not yet retaliated against us for rescuing him, but we think they will." He looked around the room, meeting eyes here and there. "We think they have already done worse, as you know." He looked saddened. Ivy, the mother of the missing twins, was not in the council room: the fate of the boys weighed heavy on them all.

"We've stayed here for generations, and we've made a home. But I believe it's time to make a move. I believe that we need to go to Salishan. Daniel, his daughter, Rachel, Pathik, Fisher, and I will leave tomorrow to fetch Daniel's wife. When we return, I will be making a new home."

A buzz of conversation began and grew louder. Some people shook their heads, some nodded, some looked deep in thought. All of them focused on Indigo again when he spoke.

"I know that it's hard to think about leaving here. We've built a place where we've felt safe, and where we can survive. But we need to do better than survive.

"We've discussed the idea of going to Salishan many times. We've argued about whether it's true there are Others there, and maybe those are just firetales. But even if there is no one there, even if Salishan is deserted, it affords us a place we can defend. It allows us the chance to build another home, a better home, where we might be able to live without fear." Indigo studied the ground in front of him for a moment. When he looked up, he looked to Rachel the way a leader should look, strong, and sure.

"When we return from our trek, I will be going to Salishan. Any who wish to join me are welcome." With that, Indigo strode out of the room.

CHAPTER 15

THEY LEFT EARLY in the morning. They set out with no fanfare. A few people were up to see them off, but most of the camp still slumbered. Rachel noticed Serena was one of those voicing farewells. She felt tempted to ask her to lessen a feeling or two—she hadn't slept all night because every time she closed her eyes she saw Peter's bloody hand, and the baern that had killed him. The baern, and others like it, were still out there.

"You look pretty tired." Her father ruffled her hair.

Rachel just nodded. She didn't want him to see that she was afraid.

"Listen," he said. "I know that this is a big responsibility, but I was hoping you would be in charge of this." He reached into his pocket and brought out the laser saw. "I've just gotten so used to a knife that this thing doesn't feel natural."

Rachel took it, feeling the smooth, deadly weight of it.

"You can tell I'm scared, can't you?" She didn't want to look at him.

"Well, I'm scared too, Rachel." He stood close. "We both saw what happened to Peter. We both know that that baern and other things like it are out there. I think if we weren't scared, I'd have to wonder how smart we were."

She finally looked at him. He was smiling. "We'll be okay."

Rachel shoved the laser saw into her pocket. She thought about what Ms. Moore had told her, before she had Crossed. That brave people are always scared. That you have to be afraid before you *can* be brave.

Daniel patted her on the back and walked over to Indigo, who was saying good-bye to Malgam and Nandy. They were staying, to get things ready for the trek to Salishan. Rachel tried to focus on the smooth shape of the laser saw and breathed deep.

As it turned out, the trek was relatively uneventful. In fact, parts of it were almost fun. They had enough food, and there was no sign of baerns. As each day passed, Rachel felt more at ease and closer to home. She and Pathik and Fisher took charge of gathering wood each night when they camped, and once they'd had their evening meal, Indigo would clear his throat and tell a firetale. He had all kinds. Some were about the first generation of survivors from when the Line was activated; how they suffered and persevered, how they despaired when all their babies were stillborn; the joy when the first baby lived, the first child born with a gift. He told a funny firetale about stumbling upon Daniel in the woods, wandering around sick as a lamb and wild-eyed, and how Daniel had thought he was a ghost of some sort. And there were tales of Salishan; of bountiful land, and safety; of miraculously undestroyed power sources—according to legend the island had been the site of a wind farm—and of Others who had somehow been able to reach the island. There were supposed to be boats abandoned on a shore not too far from the Others' camp, awaiting those who wanted passage.

Rachel loved the firetales, imagining the people in them, and the places. On the night before they were due to reach The Property, he told a firetale about the greenhouse on Ms. Moore's property. Pathik and Fisher had heard it before, but Rachel never had, and neither, it seemed, had Daniel.

"I remember it was night when we first came close to the Line. The lights were on in the greenhouse, and none of us had ever seen anything so beautiful before. The glass glittered, and the orchids inside were lush jewels. The men with me, well, boys really, we were all so young then, were amazed. As was I, of course, but I was about to see something even more amazing."

Pathik tilted his head, puzzled. He'd heard the firetale many times, but this part was new.

"She was wearing a blue dress." Indigo's face softened and his eyes focused on something far away. "Her hair was golden, and floated around her face, lit like a halo. She came out of the greenhouse alone, and walked toward the meadow where we hid. She stood there in the night, and looked so lovely, and so lonely."

"It was Ms. Moore," Rachel breathed, entranced.

Indigo smiled and looked at Pathik. "It was," he said softly. "It was your grandmother, Pathik. You'll get to meet her tomorrow."

Pathik laughed. "We've already met, in a way. She was holding a stunner, and she looked pretty fierce. At least that's what I thought I saw from where I was cowering in the bushes." He shared a look with Rachel, remembering the night she had tried to bring him the medicine his father needed.

She laughed too. "She's not someone you want mad at you."

Daniel crinkled his brow. "She has a stunner? Those are illegal for civilians, or at least they used to be."

That sent Rachel into a fit of giggles. "Ms. Moore doesn't think much of that law. You'll like her, Dad."

"So, did you *know* right then that you loved her?" Fisher was rapt, picturing the young lady lit up in the night that Indigo had described.

Indigo grew sober. "I think I may have, Fisher. I think I may have known that, right then."

"What happened to the boys that were with you, Indigo?" Rachel stirred the last of the fire's embers with a stick.

"Ah. The tale turns to a sad one there. Best to save that for some other night." Indigo rose and stretched. "These old bones are ready for sleep."

Fisher and Rachel had first watch together that night. As the rest of the camp dozed, they sat at the dying fire.

"Rachel." Fisher spoke very softly. "Have you thought about what happens when we all get back to camp?"

"What do you mean?"

"Do you and your parents plan to go with Indigo to Salishan?" Fisher kept his eyes on the forest.

"We'll go." Rachel wondered if she was supposed to be telling people. "At least I think we will. What about you?"

Fisher shook his head. "Michael will stay, so I will stay."

"Because you owe him somehow?"

Fisher looked at her then. "What do you mean?"

"Because he raised you. Or is it something else?"

"Like what?"

"Pathik seems to think you're ambitious."

Fisher grinned. "He does, doesn't he?" He spent a moment scanning the darkness beyond the glow of the embers. "I can't blame him; I used to be."

"Not anymore?"

Fisher didn't really answer her. "I'll stay in part because I owe Michael. But mostly, I'll stay because I fear Michael, or at least what Michael might lead us to. He wants us powerful, and without Indigo and Malgam here to lead, we may forget that power isn't everything."

"You mean how he wants to use the gifts against the Roberts?"

"Yes." Fisher motioned for Rachel to be quiet; he'd heard something. He stared at a particular spot at the meadow's edge for a minute. When he heard no more, he continued. "Michael doesn't think, sometimes. I asked him once how we would be different from Regs—I mean the Regs who abandoned us to our fate here—if we started using our gifts to kill. He didn't even understand the question."

"But what can you do, if you stay?"

"I don't know."

THE NEXT MORNING, they arrived at the campsite Pathik had stayed at while trying to make contact with someone at The Property. Rachel had stayed one night there, with him and the other boys on their way to his camp, after she Crossed.

Rachel eyed the black remains of the tiny fire they had made that night, and tried to believe it had only been a few weeks before. It seemed like she hadn't seen her mother or Ms. Moore for ages. She couldn't wait to get back to The Property.

"The hut is west of here." Rachel knew that they had to go to the little brick maintenance hut at the edge of The Property to use the key. Jonathan had gone there with Ms. Moore's key when she had Crossed into Away. That seemed like so long ago.

It wasn't a long hike. The little hut squatted on the field, half on The Property, half Away. A bare line of dirt where the Line prevented the field grass from growing stretched out on either side. Rachel had seen it many times from the other side. There was a rusted padlock hanging from the door hasp. She imagined Jonathan had broken that lock, when he disarmed the Line for her to Cross.

She gasped when she saw it from where she stood now. There was no door. There was nothing but a blank brick wall.

"How do we get in to use the key?" Pathik stared at the brick wall.

"Of course," said Rachel, mostly to herself. "Why would there be a door? They put this section up so fast, they didn't plan."

Daniel stepped forward. "I'll claw those bricks out if I have to."

"No need." Indigo walked up to the hut. His fingers traced the bricks, testing the mortar. When he found what he was looking for, he took out his knife and began to chip away. The mortar turned to dust.

"What?" Fisher joined Indigo. "It's mud! Dried mud."

"This is how we Crossed, the boys and I, years ago." Indigo removed the brick he'd been working on. "We put them back with mud, just as you say, Fisher."

In a very few minutes, there was a hole in the hut wall big enough for Rachel to squeeze through. She dropped to the floor inside the hut, and took the key Daniel handed through the hole to her. When she turned around she could see the door across from her, but when she reached out to touch it, the invisible barrier of the Line prevented her. It split the little hut in two.

"Do you see the key slot?" Indigo's voice came through the hole.

Rachel looked around. She was in what was basically an empty room. The only thing in it was a flat metal box, mounted to one side wall. The box spanned both sides of the Line, and it was lit on the top. Rachel walked over to it.

"Yes, I see it." She could see where the key would fit, in a slot on her side. There was an identical slot on the other side. She stood, silent, staring at the box. She wondered what her father was feeling, outside the little hut, waiting to Cross back into his life, after so many years of thinking it was over. She wondered what Pathik and Fisher would think of her world. She thought of Ms. Moore, and how she would feel when she saw Indigo. But mostly, Rachel missed her mother, and she wanted to go home.

She shoved the key into the slot.

CHAPTER 16

RACHEL LED THEM to the guesthouse, taking care to stay out of sight of the greenhouse windows. It looked empty; Vivian must be working in the main house. Daniel looked around the front room of the guesthouse with an expression on his face that Rachel couldn't decipher. She looked too, trying to see what it was he might be seeing. The yellow glass lamp on the table, the crocheted throw on the couch. The book of short stories she and her mother had been reading when she left was still on the table near the lamp, a scrap of paper marking their place. It felt like she had been gone from this room, gone from all its comforts, for years instead of weeks.

"You lived here?" Daniel touched the back of the couch. He looked like he wanted to touch everything in the room, to soak up all of the years he had missed with his wife and child. He looked like he knew he could never do it.

"Yes." Rachel went to him. "It wasn't bad."

Daniel nodded. He kept his eyes on the couch.

"Where is your mother?" Indigo sounded uneasy. His eyes kept shifting toward the door.

"She's working. I'll go and find her. You should all stay inside until we come back."

She turned to go, and ran straight into Pathik, who was wide-eyed, staring at a digim that was sitting next to the lamp. It was one of the few digimations they had; most of theirs were old-fashioned, static 3-D digims. But a few months before Rachel Crossed, Vivian had splurged on a new imager. The digim Pathik was staring at had been taken with that, and it showed Rachel laughing, on a loop. Her head came up, revealing her face, and she giggled at her mother, who had been practicing with the new imager. Then it repeated. The sound was off, but Rachel could remember Vivian laughing back, and telling her to stand still. They had had a lot of fun that evening.

"That's you." Pathik looked from the digim to Rachel.

"Yes." Rachel couldn't help smiling at the astonishment in his voice. Pathik smiled, and shook his head at his own incredulousness.

"What makes it move?"

Rachel shrugged. "I don't really know how it works."

"Doesn't matter right now." Fisher sounded irritated. "We have things to do."

"He's right," said Daniel. "You should go, Rachel. Be careful. If it's safe, bring your mom back here."

Pathik was still staring at the digimation when she left.

* * *

THE GREENHOUSE WAS empty. She wished she had time to check on the orchid crosses she had germinated before she left, just to see if they were doing okay, but she didn't think she dared. It was close to lunchtime, so she was betting that Vivian and Ms. Moore were in the main house. Jonathan might be in town, or working on some other part of The Property.

She paused by some bushes, watching the front door of the main house and listening for anything coming toward the house from the long driveway. It all seemed quiet, as it would on any normal day. She ran to the grand porch and stood hugging one of the huge columns, as though it could hide her. Still nothing. There had once been a time when coming to the main house for any reason had made her almost this nervous, but that was back when she was afraid of Ms. Moore. She'd seen a different side of her before she Crossed. Now she was afraid *for* Ms. Moore. For all of them.

She took a deep breath and scurried from the column to the front door. She hit the intercom buzzer and waited. For a couple of moments nothing happened, but then she heard the hollow click that meant somebody was pressing the intercom on the other side of the door.

"Yes?"

It was her mother's voice.

"Mom." The word stuck in her suddenly dry throat. She licked her lips and started to repeat it. Before she could, the door swung open, and there was Vivian, wide-eyed, tears already streaming down her cheeks. She grabbed Rachel and held her, rocking her where they stood. Rachel felt her own tears filling her eyes.

"Inside. Inside right now." Ms. Moore appeared, and scooted them both off the porch. For some time there was nothing but sniffling and hugging.

"Oh." Ms. Moore stood back from Rachel and Vivian and put her hand on her chest. "I swear I cannot take any more." She smiled, and dabbed at her eyes with the linen handkerchief she always had in a pocket. "Let's all go into the parlor, shall we? We were just having some kalitea—I'll get another cup from the pantry."

"I'll get it," said Vivian, but she was silenced by a look from Ms. Moore.

Rachel followed Vivian into the parlor and sat on the couch with her. Ms. Moore returned with a third china cup, and poured kalitea for all of them. Vivian just kept staring at Rachel, and touching her hair. Rachel didn't mind.

"Well?" Ms. Moore could not contain herself any longer. "Is my son—is Malgam alive?" She laughed, a slightly hysterical laugh. "I mean no disrespect, of course, Vivian. But we see Rachel is fine, and thank goodness for that. I just need to know . . ."

"It's all right." Vivian leaned across the table and patted Ms. Moore's hand. "I understand completely."

"He's okay." Rachel smiled. "He took the antibiotics and

he got better. They have a healer there, but she couldn't help him. The medicine you sent did. And he's okay." She turned to Vivian. "Mom." She couldn't go on.

Vivian's joyful expression turned grave in an instant. She took both of Rachel's hands in hers. "Rachel. No matter what happened to you, you're here now, and you're safe. We can get you through whatever it—"

"No, Mom." Rachel squeezed Vivian's hands. "It's nothing like that."

She wasn't sure how to tell Vivian that her husband, the man she thought had been dead since Rachel was three, was sitting on the couch in the guesthouse right that moment. She wasn't sure how to tell Ms. Moore that the man she lost so many years ago, the father of her child, Malgam, was probably sitting on the same couch, along with her grandson. She decided to just blurt it out.

"Dad and Indigo and Pathik are in the guesthouse."

Vivian said nothing. Ms. Moore said nothing. Rachel waited. She knew it was a lot to process. While she waited for the questions she was sure would come, she noticed the sugar on the kalitea tray and helped herself to two spoons of it. She stirred it up and sipped. Sugar. It seemed like she hadn't had any sugar forever. It made the kalitea syrupy and smooth on her tongue. It was heavenly.

She realized it was still silent in the room, and glanced up. Her mother and Ms. Moore were staring at her as though her ears were flapping back and forth.

"Did you say *Dad*?" Vivian's mouth was open. Rachel

nodded. She had never seen her mom so shocked, and she was almost afraid to say anything more.

"Your father is alive?" Vivian touched her own hair unconsciously—the red hair Daniel had always loved, the hair she had refused to cut or color even when she knew it would be wise to alter her appearance, back in the days right after they fled to The Property. She had always thought, in the back of her mind, that he might see it, might find her, even though she knew, all those years, that he was dead.

"He thought we were dead, Mom." Rachel wasn't sure what the expression on Vivian's face signified. "He had someone check. They couldn't find us, and they assumed we had been Identified and hauled off. That's what they told Dad."

Vivian was up and out of the room before any more could be said. Rachel started to go after her, but Ms. Moore motioned her back to her seat.

"Let her go to him."

"Indigo's there too." Rachel wasn't certain Ms. Moore had heard.

"Yes. I'm certain your mother will bring him along." Ms. Moore's tone didn't invite more discussion on the subject. "Are you all right, Rachel? Nobody hurt you, did they?"

"No. They didn't." Rachel felt so tired. She was here. Safe. With her mother and Ms. Moore. She wanted to sleep. For hours. And then shower in hot, hot water. Instead, she drank her sugary kalitea. She knew it would be a long time before she slept.

"What's going on?" Jonathan came into the parlor, pushing back the brim of his hat. "I just saw Ms. Quillen running to the guesthouse like—" He broke off, and stared at Rachel, shocked. "Child!" His chin began to tremble in an odd way, and Rachel realized he was holding back tears. She went to him and hugged him. She wasn't surprised at how glad she was to see him. He had been like a grandfather to her in so many ways while she grew up on The Property.

"I'm okay," she whispered in his ear. He hugged her back, and then held her at arm's length for inspection.

"My dad's here. And Indigo." Rachel hugged him again. She didn't see how Jonathan's smile faltered slightly.

"Well," said Jonathan softly. "It sounds like you have a story to tell."

They sat down on the couch together and talked. Ms. Moore went for another cup, and poured Jonathan some kalitea. Then Rachel told them about Away.

WHEN THE DOOR to the guesthouse burst open, instantly four knives were drawn and at the ready. Vivian didn't hesitate at the sight of the blades pointed in her direction. She scanned the faces of the people before her. In three of them she saw many things: fear, curiosity, fatigue. But there was a fourth, and in the fourth face, Vivian saw her life.

He looked so old. But she could see him so clearly, through the scars and the roughened skin, the lines and the shadows. There he was. Alive.

"Daniel." She meant to say it out loud, but her mouth formed the word without sound. She saw one of the others—an old man—gesture to the two boys to retreat.

He came to her, like she had imagined so many times that he might. But his hand in hers was warm, and his tears wet her cheek when he kissed her. This was real, not a dream. And she knew she would never be parted from him again.

RACHEL FIELDED QUESTION after question. Ms. Moore and Jonathan wanted to know every detail of the past weeks: how Away was, what the Others' camp was like, how many survivors there were. After what seemed like a long time to Rachel, they heard the front door open quietly. Daniel and Vivian walked into the parlor arm in arm, followed by Indigo, Pathik, and Fisher. Vivian's eyes were red, but her face was filled with light. She could not stop smiling. Daniel seemed to be having a hard time taking his eyes off her.

The two boys gawked like tourists, their curiosity over-coming any sense of caution. Indigo looked around too, but his eyes halted at the digim on the mantel. It was of him, as a young man. His gaze went from the digim to Ms. Moore.

"Elizabeth." He whispered her name. She got to her feet, somewhat unsteadily. Rachel stepped around the table and took her arm.

"Thank you, Rachel." Ms. Moore sounded steadier than she looked. "I wonder if you and your mother could show the boys and Daniel where they can clean up a bit. I'd like a moment with Indigo."

"Certainly." Vivian exchanged a glance with Rachel. It was not a simple reunion for Ms. Moore. "Perhaps we should all go back to the guesthouse."

"No," said Ms. Moore. "I think we had all better stay in the main house, don't you? There are plenty of bedrooms, and it's better if we don't have to go back and forth—less chance of being seen. If there's anything you need from the guesthouse, best go and get it."

"I can go later, once it's dark. I'll turn on some lights so it looks like I've settled in for the night as usual, and then come back." Vivian held Daniel's hand in hers. "For now, if you'll follow us upstairs, boys?" She motioned to Pathik and Fisher. "Rachel and I will show you around."

"I've got some things to see to in the greenhouse," said Jonathan, his eyes on the floor. He left without another word.

There was silence. Indigo and Elizabeth stood, awkward and shy. Elizabeth stared at the floor. She couldn't bring herself to look at him.

"A rather handsome fellow, there." Indigo smiled. Elizabeth heard the smile in his voice and looked up. He pointed at the digim on the mantel.

"Isn't he, though?" Elizabeth smiled too. "I made a huge mistake when I let him go." She closed the distance between them, holding out her hands. Indigo took a deep breath, as though he were about to dive into water, exhaled, and

clasped her hands in his own. His eyes lit on her necklace—
on the band suspended there.

"You still have the ring." He smiled again.

"Of course I still have the ring." Elizabeth swallowed.
"I've learned from my mistake. I've paid for it. I won't make
another like it." Elizabeth sought his eyes, hoping to see for-
giveness there.

She did. They walked together to the sofa, and sat down.
There was so much to say. Elizabeth hoped they had forever,
now, to say it.

FISHER'S EYES WERE as round as moons. He was watching the warm water fill the sink in the guest bathroom.

"How does it get up here, inside the house?" He ran his
fingers along the faucet, tracing it to its base, eyeing the cabinet the base disappeared into.

"It comes from the water condensation unit and then it
goes through the heating unit and then . . . it's a long story."
Rachel chuckled. "We don't have time."

Fisher smiled. He put his hands under the water. He
watched as it slid along his fingers and dripped off into the
sink. "You're probably right." He pointed to the dispenser
on the countertop. "Is that soap, then?"

"Yes." Rachel opened a cabinet and took down several thick cotton towels. "There are more in the hall if you
need them. Just let me know." Rachel wanted to check on
Pathik.

She found him sitting on the guest bed in the third guest room. The door was ajar. Rachel sat in the chair next to the window. "Do you think they'll be all right?"

Pathik knew who she meant. He shrugged. "I hope so. I know he's always had a hard time, being without her. He's been so lonely."

"What do you mean? He's got a lot of friends. He has his family." Rachel didn't think Indigo seemed lonely. From what she had seen of him at camp, he was busy, and kind, and respected. He always had at least a few people around him.

Pathik looked away. "It's different. He had his one love. To lose that would . . ." He fell silent. When he looked back in Rachel's direction he wouldn't meet her gaze.

"I'm all done in that room." The door swung open all the way, propelled by a shove from Fisher, who squinted at Pathik when he saw his face.

"You all right, Path?" The squint turned into a smirk.

Pathik glared at Fisher and stood. He pushed past him without another word and left the room.

Rachel glared at Fisher too.

"What?" His smile got wider. "I just asked if he was all right."

"It's time to eat." Vivian leaned in the doorway. "We have a feast downstairs."

"Pathik's still in the bathroom," said Rachel. "I can wait for him."

"Never mind that," said Fisher. "You ladies go on ahead.

I can fetch Pathik down when he's done preening. We'll find you fine."

"Come on, Rachel." Vivian held out both hands. "Your dad is waiting for you." Her smile was like a sunlit bloom, warm and beautiful. Rachel stood and took her hands, but she shot Fisher a look over her shoulder.

Downstairs the dining room table had been set with all the best china and glassware. Either Ms. Moore or Vivian had set out candles and lit them; Rachel grinned at the irony of that. The Others would be much more impressed if they just left all the electric lights on. Rachel thought of all the forced employee holiday meals she had endured here, when she was still afraid of Ms. Moore, and thought of her as a mean old woman. The same translucent plates and delicate crystal goblets, but Rachel felt no fear of breaking them. She only felt tired, and happy, and home.

CHAPTER 17

INDIGO SAT AT the head of the table, with Ms. Moore to his right. Dinner, for something thrown together more hastily than Vivian was used to, was a fine affair. There was grilled salmon, homemade biscuits and honey, fresh greens, brown rice steamed tender with butter and salt, wine, and orange juice from the last can Vivian had been able to find in Bensen. She'd been saving it in the freezer for something, since long before Rachel Crossed. She thought maybe tonight was the something.

The men fell silent as the dishes were brought out and set on the table, as though something holy was occurring. Rachel knew why. Food wasn't exactly scarce Away, but it wasn't plentiful either. And spices like the ones Vivian had used on the salmon didn't exist there. There was salt. The Others used small peppers and onions to flavor other foods. But they didn't have cayenne, or nutmeg, or brown sugar. Vivian used those in a marinade she brushed on salmon steaks; it was one of Rachel's favorites.

At first, there was very little talk. Vivian and Elizabeth seemed content to just watch the men eat. Rachel was busy eating, herself. Soon, though, appetites were blunted. Indigo was the first to sit back and heave a deep sigh.

"That was so delicious."

"Surely you aren't finished?" Ms. Moore sounded heartbroken.

"Not at all," said Indigo, patting his stomach. "Just taking a break. And while I do, I think we should probably discuss some things."

Pathik and Fisher both put their forks down, with a mournful air. Indigo chuckled.

"Boys, no need to stop—we can talk and enjoy this wonderful meal at the same time."

Ms. Moore smiled at him, looking as happy as Rachel had ever imagined seeing her look.

"I think we need to pack whatever we can and Cross," said Vivian. She was looking at Daniel, but the image of the bloodstained grate inside the government vehicle kept appearing in her mind.

"I agree," said Indigo. "I hope," he said, reaching out to take Ms. Moore's hand, "that we all agree. It may seem frightening to think of Crossing, but it's not safe here."

Ms. Moore covered his hand with hers. "We will. This time, we will."

"This is so good," said Fisher, pointing to his salmon. "Can we take some of whatever spice this is with us?"

Everyone laughed.

"Actually, that's not a bad idea," said Pathik. "There are all kinds of things we can use to improve life. Just a small thing like that laser saw made a huge difference."

"I'd be dead if Rachel hadn't had that," said Daniel. "I'm told I have you to thank for that, Ms. Moore."

"Call me Elizabeth, please." Ms. Moore smiled at Daniel. "I think we need to make a list. Medicine, more solar-powered tools, spices. What else can we come up with? We'll get what we can in the morning and leave tomorrow night. We shouldn't waste any more time than that."

"What about Peter's wife? What about his daughter? We have to at least try to help them." Rachel wondered how they could help them, even as she asked the questions.

"Oh Rachel." Vivian looked sorrowful. "Your dad told me about Peter. He really was our friend after all, wasn't he?" She hesitated. "Jolie and Trina were listed as dead in yesterday's streamer news, Rachel."

"Are you sure?" Rachel knew the answer before Vivian's somber nod confirmed it.

"They listed them as infected with one of the viruses. Nobody thinks twice about that anymore. There's always a new one that the drugs can't kill."

Every few years there was a new flu, one that killed a few thousand people a day for a few weeks, until the government came up with a drug that stopped it. Rachel had never given the death lists a thought; it was just a part of life. Now she wondered how many of those deaths weren't from viruses.

"All the more reason to get out of here." Daniel looked angry.

"We'll have to get what we need from Bensen if I don't have it here. Medicines, maybe some of the tools," said Ms. Moore.

"What about asking Dr. Beller?" Rachel was confused. When they had been readying supplies to pass on to Pathik, Dr. Beller had delivered medicine and other medical items to The Property, in return for a large sum. He had been Ms. Moore's doctor for years; he'd helped her when Malgam was born, and hadn't reported the baby to the authorities or questioned why Ms. Moore didn't want Malgam's genids recorded at the birth.

"Dr. Beller died, Rachel," said Ms. Moore. "Right after he brought the medical supplies out last time, he had a heart attack, or at least that's what was reported. We'll have to chance the black market in Bensen to get medical supplies now."

Jonathan had been quiet during the meal, passing dishes and pouring wine, but now he spoke.

"I think I should go alone, and get the things you'll need. I know where some of the backdoor vendors can be found. And there's less chance of someone being suspicious than if a band of strangers ends up in town."

"You're probably right about that, Jonathan." Daniel nodded. "That's very generous of you to offer."

Elizabeth studied Jonathan. "You said the supplies *we* will need. Aren't you coming with us?"

Everyone was silent. Jonathan didn't say anything for a long time. When he did speak, it was more to Daniel than to Elizabeth.

"I figure you might need a contact on this side. You never know. And I'm an old man. It's too late for me to start over."

"No." Rachel shook her head. "No, Jonathan. You have to come with us. The EOs will know something happened when Mom and Ms. Moore just disappear. They won't leave you alone. You have to come." Rachel's hands were both squeezed into fists.

"All I have to say is that I reported for work in the morning and Ms. Moore and your mom were gone. They won't trouble with me. Not much, anyway." Jonathan reached over and touched Rachel's shoulder. She shook his hand off.

"It *is* a better idea for Jonathan to go alone to Bensen." Ms. Moore sounded very tired. Or perhaps just very sad. "As for the rest of it, we'll talk more later. For now, our list. And then I suggest we all retire. We'll need our rest."

"WHAT'S THE PROBLEM with Jonathan?" Pathik was sitting in the upstairs landing with Rachel. They had to wait in line to get ready for bed, because there were only two bathrooms in the main house, and seven people. Jonathan had gone back to his own home for the night; he would return very early in the morning to get creds and the list of supplies before he headed for Bensen. Ms. Moore was already in bed—she had gone to her room right after dinner. Vivian and Daniel were tidying downstairs and Fisher and Indigo were washing up.

"He's going to come with us. He has to." Rachel was still upset at the thought that Jonathan might stay behind.

"He used to love Ms. Moore, didn't he?" Pathik spoke so quietly he was almost whispering.

Rachel stared at him. "Did you feel that? Did you feel it with your gift?"

Pathik nodded. "Not that I would have to use my gift. It was plain on his face. He used to love her and she loved Indigo. Right?"

"I think he still loves her," said Rachel.

Pathik shook his head. "He loves her, but not like that, not anymore."

"You don't know that for sure." Rachel knew he did, though.

Pathik ignored her comment. "It must have been hard for him, knowing she loved someone else, when he felt so much for her."

"I guess." Rachel frowned. She'd been wondering about Pathik's gift. She'd never asked him exactly how it worked. "When you feel other people's emotions . . . do you know what they're thinking? Like Jonathan, do you hear what he thinks about Ms. Moore?"

Pathik shrugged. "It's not like that. It's more like, well, like colors. Or maybe like temperatures?" He thought. "It's like the emotions people are feeling, emotions that they might not even be aware of themselves, just frame what they say—put it in context. So if someone says 'I'm telling you the truth' but the emotion they are feeling is fear or anger, they may not really be telling the truth." He looked frustrated. "That's a bad example. It's much more subtle than that, more involved, but I can't really explain it."

"So you don't really hear what someone is thinking."

"No."

"But you can tell what they are feeling."

"If I look, yes, I can."

"And what's the rule on that?" Rachel cast him a sidelong glance. "Does Usage prohibit you from looking without permission?"

Pathik grinned at her. "Yes. But sometimes, I can't help it. There's spillover, and even without trying I can just . . . tell."

Rachel didn't say anything. She looked at her hands in her lap.

Pathik changed the subject. "How is Jonathan going to get to Bensen tomorrow?"

"He'll probably take his vehicle. He has a truck. Ms. Moore's utility vehicle might hold more stuff, but he never drives it. If anyone was watching, it would look strange for him to take that." Rachel tilted her head at Pathik. "Why?"

"I want to go to Bensen." Pathik held up his hand to stop her protest. "I know, I know. But I'll never have a chance to see anything like it again in my life, Rachel. I just want to go look."

"Jonathan will never take you."

"He's got to come inside to get the list. I could hide in the truck, couldn't I?"

Rachel shook her head.

"I'll stay hidden, Rachel." Pathik pleaded.

Rachel shook her head some more. But she thought about the tarp Jonathan always had in the back of his truck.

"He'll find you, the minute he loads anything into the back."

"By then it will be too late to do anything about it." A door opened down the hall and Pathik dropped his voice to a whisper. "Please."

Rachel scowled. "I'll only do it if I come too."

Pathik shook his head. "It's not safe for you to—" He stopped talking. The look on Rachel's face was fierce. No words were required.

Footsteps sounded in the hall and Fisher came around the corner.

"Washroom is free." Fisher's face was shiny clean. "I love that soap."

Rachel and Pathik both laughed at his dreamy expression. Rachel stood.

"I'll go next." She gave Pathik a pointed look. "See you in the morning."

CHAPTER 18

IT WAS A gray, chilly dawn. Rachel and Pathik had snuck out of the house early and hidden in the bushes along the driveway. When Jonathan arrived they watched him enter the house. He left the truck running; he must have planned to dash inside and right back out. Rachel motioned for Pathik to climb in the back. She hopped in herself.

"I really think it's a bad idea for you to come." Pathik whispered, although nobody could hear them from inside the house.

Rachel just shrugged. "At least the tarp isn't folded—he would notice if it was folded when he went in and unfolded when he came back." She crawled underneath it. "Come on, we don't have forever here."

Pathik heaved an exasperated sigh. "Scoot over." He settled next to her and they both tried to make their bodies as small as possible. "Tuck in your foot."

"Oh, tuck in your own foot," said Rachel. "I seriously cannot believe you are making me do this."

"I just wanted some help sneaking out. I'm not making you come along."

The front door opened and they heard Jonathan's voice. After a few minutes they heard the truck door open and the truck moved; it dipped a bit as Jonathan climbed in the driver's seat. The truck door closed.

"Hold on," breathed Rachel. She laughed, as softly as she could, at the look on Pathik's face when they took off. It was hard for her to remember sometimes that he didn't have the same range of experiences she did; he had never ridden in a vehicle. The fastest he had ever gone was as fast as he could run.

They didn't talk during the ride. At one point they hit a particularly large pot hole and Rachel was tossed hard; Pathik caught her around the waist and kept her from hitting the truck's side panel. When she started to settle herself away from him again, he kept his arm around her. The rest of the ride to Bensen was a blur. Pathik's arm around her waist felt so warm, and Rachel found she couldn't turn and look at him. Somehow, even without looking, she knew he was grinning.

Soon enough they slowed; Rachel knew that meant they were coming into town. She leaned over and spoke into Pathik's ear.

"Don't move or make a noise until Jonathan's gone. Once it's totally quiet I'll peek first. Got it?"

Pathik's cheeks flushed as she whispered; when Rachel saw that, she grinned.

They waited, frozen. Jonathan got out of the truck; it rose again without his weight. When they heard the truck door shut she could feel Pathik tense; she put her hand on his arm and shook her head.

After she had heard nothing for a full minute, Rachel found the edge of the tarp and peeked out. She couldn't see anything but the truck bed.

"Wait," she hissed to Pathik, though he hadn't moved. Then she stretched up higher until she could see past the walls of the bed. They were parked on a side street; that made sense. Jonathan wouldn't have parked on the main street, where everyone could see his truck. Most of the places he had to go probably weren't on the main street anyway; they were selling things illegally.

"Okay." Rachel uncovered Pathik's head. "There's not that much to see, really. We're on a side street of the town."

"The buildings are so new. And smooth too." Pathik looked around as wide-eyed as a child.

"Get down!" Rachel pulled him closer and pulled the tarp over them. A man was coming up the street. They listened to his footsteps on the pavement. When they couldn't hear anything, Rachel peeked again. "Okay." She uncovered them again.

"Will we go anywhere else in town?"

"I don't know," said Rachel. "I don't know if Jonathan can walk to where he needs to go from here, or if he needs to come back and move the truck. I'd imagine not, though. Bensen isn't that big."

Pathik's face fell a bit. He was hoping to see more than the backs of some buildings. They waited, watching carefully for anyone who might pass by. Nobody else did.

"Rachel." Pathik had stopped looking at the buildings at some point and started looking at Rachel. She had felt his gaze, but she had been too shy to return it. Now she looked at him. He wasn't smiling.

"I know we haven't had a chance really to talk about it." Pathik took a deep breath. He looked down at his hands. Rachel couldn't decipher his expression; he looked almost as though he was in some sort of physical pain. "At least, we *haven't* talked about it."

"Talked about what?" Rachel was concerned now. She'd never seen Pathik this way.

"At first I told myself I wasn't saying anything to you because you might prefer Fisher."

"Fisher?" Rachel didn't understand.

"You know he's interested in you." Pathik gauged her expression. "You mean you didn't know?"

"No!" Rachel couldn't believe she'd been so oblivious. When she thought back, she could see where it might be true. "I had no idea."

"Well," said Pathik. "Now you do." He stared at his shoes.

"What would his being interested in me stop you from saying to me?"

"Nothing, really. I just used that for an excuse. I *have*

been afraid. But not of competition from Fisher. I've been thinking of Indigo, and my father and your father, and that's what I've always thought of when I think of love. How people *lose* their love."

Pathik bit his lip. He looked square at her. "I haven't thought enough about how people might *find* love. Like my father did, with Nandy. Or like your father did, with your mother. Or like Indigo has, again, with Ms. Moore. With my grandmother." He smiled as he said the word *grandmother*. "It doesn't always have to be loss."

Rachel nodded. She knew what he meant about equating love with pain and loss. She thought she must have felt that way forever, or at least as long as she and her mother had been without her father.

"Do you think it really can be . . . something good?"

He answered without words. He reached for her hand and brought it to his lips. He kissed her palm, and the world turned quiet, as though there was nothing but the back of the truck, and Pathik. He leaned toward her, and she had never felt anything so warm when he kissed her mouth. She closed her eyes and returned the soft pressure of his lips, and wondered why she hadn't done this sooner. Kissing. It was lovely.

But then her head was yanked backward, with a force so rough it felt like her neck might snap. She screamed in pain; someone had hold of her hair and it felt like they were trying to drag her from the back of the truck. She scratched blindly backward, but she couldn't loosen the grip on her hair.

"No!" She heard Pathik yell, and saw him leap over her, throwing himself at her attacker. The grip on her hair released. In the seconds it took her to sit up Pathik had landed enough blows to bloody the man. It was a stranger—a rough-looking man, older than Pathik by ten years or so. Rachel had a fleeting thought about all the times her mother had cautioned her to stay close on their trips to Bensen; young girls disappeared every day in the cities, and even in Bensen men like this weren't unknown.

The man tried to run, but Pathik's fury seemed endless. He kept hitting the man, the blows landing with a sound that made Rachel wince. Finally, the man was able to stumble out of Pathik's reach. He ran for the main street.

"Pathik—" Before she could say more, Pathik pushed her down roughly. His eyes looked wild. There was blood on his lip.

"Hide." He whispered the word at the same time that a shout rang out behind him. It didn't come from the stranger.

"Halt!" It was an EO.

Anguish crumpled Pathik's mouth. He focused upon her face for an instant, and then she could see his gaze turn inward. "Hide, Rachel." He turned and ran away from the truck.

She pulled the tarp up. And listened. At first there was nothing, but then she heard Pathik cry out. Rachel hugged herself, and tried to be still. Tears streamed silently down her cheeks.

"Told you to halt, fool." The EO sounded winded. Rachel heard footsteps, coming fast, then stopping.

"What's this?" Another EO.

"Fight," said the first, and a possible vehicle prowl. "One ran away, but this one seemed ready to try to get into that truck."

"Scan him yet?"

"About to. I had to stun him. He wouldn't stop."

There was no more talking for a minute. Rachel knew the EOs were scanning Pathik for his genid, to see who he was. She knew they wouldn't find a listing for him. In the U.S., every child's genetic identity was scanned at birth and entered into the national registry. But Pathik had been born Away. There would be nothing in their system.

"Hmmm."

"What?"

"He's not coming up."

"What do you mean he's not coming up? They just went through the registry for errors. If he has a genid he's going to come up."

"I know." The first EO sounded irritated. "I'm telling you he's not coming up."

"Cuff him." The second EO sounded afraid. "Quick! Wrists *and* ankles. I'll go get the vehicle. We gotta take this guy in."

"What about the truck? Should I run it?"

"If he was about to break into it, it's not his truck. Just watch him close until I come back."

Rachel squeezed her eyes shut, trying to stop the tears. She hugged herself tighter under the tarp, listening to the sounds of the EOs' vehicle approaching, of Pathik being roughly lifted and put in the back. The door slammed. Two more door slams and the vehicle left.

She waited several minutes, listening, afraid to move. She knew she had to get out of the truck. Finally she just threw back the tarp and sat up. Just in time to see a man walking toward her. She was crying so hard that his image wavered; she could make out a hat and it looked like he was carrying a bag. He saw her and stopped in place. Rachel started to climb out of the truck, but her foot caught and she fell out instead. She landed on her side. As she tried to scramble up she heard the man running toward her. She scrambled under the truck, waiting for him to get closer. As soon as he tried to reach for her she would get out the other side.

"Child."

It was Jonathan.

CHAPTER 19

SHE WAS ATTACKED, most likely a flesh trader looking for merchandise. The boy saved her, but then the EOs came."

Rachel sat on the parlor couch, despondent. Everyone was there, listening to Jonathan tell what had happened in town. Her mother was so upset that she could barely speak to her. Her father had made certain she was unhurt and then turned his attention quickly to Jonathan. Ms. Moore and Indigo looked stricken, and Fisher looked like he could not believe her idiocy.

"We have to get him out of there." Ms. Moore was near tears.

"But how, exactly?" Vivian knew what Ms. Moore was thinking and she knew she was probably right; Pathik was in some cell, where very bad things were going to happen to him. She didn't know how they would ever get him out of it.

"Will he be in Bensen?" Indigo spoke calmly. "Or will they take him to a bigger city?"

"They will probably take him to Ganivar, once they discover he really doesn't have a genid." Daniel looked worried. "Who knows where they'll take him from there. If they think he's from Away they'll send him somewhere for testing. Somewhere with high security. I think if we're going to move, we have to move now." He turned to Ms. Moore. "Do you have any weapons?"

"I have a stunner. Only one."

"That may be enough." Indigo took Ms. Moore's hand.

"They have lots of stunners. One won't make a bit of difference," said Jonathan.

"We can trade for him," said Indigo.

"You mean the maps?" Ms. Moore felt hope stirring for the first time since she saw that Pathik wasn't with Jonathan and Rachel. "We can trade the maps. They'll want those."

Indigo started to say something, but Daniel interrupted. "She's right. Pathik's more important than the maps."

"That's very true. But I was going to say—"

"I didn't bring them." Rachel sounded miserable. "I thought they would be safer at camp. I left them with Nandy."

"They are safer there, Rachel. You made the right decision." Indigo thought for a moment. "We could trade something they *think* is the maps."

"They'll check," said Vivian.

Indigo nodded. "Yes, they will." He looked at Ms. Moore. "I think it's worth a try. But I'll be the one to go do it."

Daniel began to protest, but Indigo shook his head. "We

have no time, Daniel, to argue. And I need you to help get everything ready. Perhaps Jonathan will be willing to drive me into town?"

"I can do that." Jonathan tipped his hat back on his forehead. "Rachel said they never ran a check on my truck, so they won't have it flagged. I bet they'll have the boy at the main Enforcement station until tomorrow, at least. Seems to take them a while to figure things out."

"Do you have anything that might pass for valuable maps, Elizabeth?"

"The printouts!" Rachel jumped up. "Remember, Ms. Moore? Your great-grandfather's?" Ms. Moore had shown Rachel some printouts that detailed the way the U.S. looked before the Line was built and activated, along with a diary that had belonged to her great-grandfather, before Rachel Crossed to get the medicine to the Others. He had been in the military and was involved in the aftermath of activating the Line.

"The rest of you get everything ready to Cross," said Indigo. "It'll need to happen fast."

"I'm so sorry," whispered Rachel. "I should have told him no."

Indigo held out his arms to Rachel. She went to him, grateful for his hug. "Pathik is his own person. You saying no wouldn't have stopped him from going." Indigo patted her back. "All will be well."

"I'm going to go get the stunner. Rachel, you know where the box with the printouts is—can you go get it?"

Ms. Moore hurried from the room, with Rachel on her heels.

Fisher had been watching Indigo intently. Now he walked over to him.

"Usage says harm no one." Fisher spoke so softly nobody but Indigo heard.

"I know what Usage says, Fisher." Indigo smiled. "I'm glad to know that you know it so well too."

Ms. Moore came back with the stunner. She showed Indigo how it worked. Rachel appeared with the maps she'd fetched from a box in the cellar. Everyone began to move toward the front door until Indigo stopped them.

"If they are watching, this crowd bursting out the front door is all it would take. Let's keep our heads." He turned to Ms. Moore. "I love you, Elizabeth. As I always have." He looked at the rest of the assembly. "Pack fast. Be calm. Be ready to Cross when you hear the truck coming back." Then he turned and walked out the door. Jonathan followed. Fisher watched them leave with a worried look on his face.

NEITHER OF THE two men said anything for the first ten minutes of the ride back to Bensen. They both seemed to be involved in their own thoughts. Jonathan was the first to speak.

"You really do love her, right?"

Indigo gave him a sidelong look. "I do."

"Why do you think she didn't go with you, back then?"

"I don't know. I think she was afraid, more afraid than she thought."

"If it helps any, I think she regrets it."

Indigo stared out at the road ahead of them. "I've always known that. And it never helped a bit."

No more was said until they reached Bensen. Jonathan parked the truck a block from the Enforcement office. He pointed the building out to Indigo.

"What's your plan?"

"Do you know the layout inside?"

Jonathan nodded. "It's a small town. The Enforcement office is the place people go to buy vehicle licenses or pay fines." He closed his eyes, picturing the interior in his mind. "All on the first floor. A reception area in front. Offices in back. Cells too. Not that I've seen the cells."

"How many officers?"

"Usually just four on a shift. Two roaming, one at the desk, one in the back. They might have called in extra men, though, for this."

Indigo looked at Jonathan. "I'm not counting on the maps to work."

"Didn't figure you were." Jonathan waited.

"If he comes out, I want you to go." Indigo watched to see if Jonathan understood.

"Want me to wait any?"

Indigo shook his head. Then he opened the truck door and got out. Jonathan watched him walk away, watched him reach the door of the Enforcement office. He stopped outside for a moment. Then he pushed the door open and disappeared.

The maps lay on the passenger seat where Indigo had left them.

CHAPTER 20

The EO BEHIND the counter looked nervous. Indigo walked straight up to him and spoke.

"You have a boy here."

"This ain't a public show, old man. Go mind your own business."

"The boy's gift won't be that useful to you."

"What are you talking about?" The EO took a closer look at Indigo. His eyes widened when he saw the crude wooden buttons on Indigo's shirt. "You're dressed like that kid." He slammed his hand down on an intercom button. "Willy, get out here."

"What?" A voice came from some hidden speaker.

"Get out here, now! There's—" The EO stopped talking as he felt the cool smooth tip of a stunner on his throat. Indigo had come around the counter.

"Stand up, slowly," said Indigo, holding the EOs neck.

They turned together to face the back, just as another EO came out.

"Drop your weapon!" The EO crouched and took out his own stunner, after shouting the order.

Indigo just looked at him. "Drop yours, or I'll kill your friend."

There was a tense silence. Finally the EO Indigo was restraining spoke.

"Drop the stunner, Willy."

"Seriously?"

"Yes."

The second EO—Willy—dropped his weapon.

"Slide it over here," said Indigo. The EO did. Indigo reached down and picked it up. He put it in his pocket. "Thank you, Willy. Now let's all go in the back."

They walked down a short hallway. There were only two doors off of it: one to an empty office and one marked HOLDING. Indigo motioned for Willy to open the door. There were two cells. A third EO was sitting outside the cell closer to them with his back to the door, arms folded in front of him, watching the sole occupant. Pathik looked bruised and his face was bloody, but he was conscious. He said nothing when he saw Indigo.

The EO in the chair spoke without turning around. "Chad'll be back with the food in a few minutes. Has the Ganivar station called back yet?"

"Don."

The EO turned in his seat. He started to unfold his arms. His mouth hung open in shock.

"Put your stunner on the floor." Indigo waited.

"My stunner's on the desk." Don indicated a small desk against the wall.

"You." Indigo spoke to Willy. "You tie that one up." He nodded his head toward Don.

"Tie him up?" The EO looked confused.

"Just cuff me, Willy. That'll do, right?" Don raised his eyebrows at Indigo.

"Yes." Indigo watched as Willy put plasticuffs on the EO's wrists. "Ankles too. And then do this one." He pointed to the man he held.

Once the two EOs were cuffed at wrists and ankles, Indigo pointed the stunner at Willy. "Open that cell."

Willy shook his head, eyes wide. "We can't let him go. He's one of those—"

"Willy!" Don sounded exasperated. "He's one of them too."

Willy's eyes got even wider. "Should I use your key, Don?"

Don nodded. Willy went to him and gingerly unclipped a flat plastic disc from his belt. He took it to the cell, where Pathik sat, silent. Willy inserted the disc into a slot on the cell door. A light blinked and the door clicked. Willy opened it.

"Pathik, step out." Indigo waited until Pathik was standing next to him. "Now, Willy, you go inside, and shut the door."

"Why don't you go inside, old man." It was a voice from behind them.

Indigo didn't turn. He kept his stunner pointed at Willy.

"I guess you must be Chad, back with lunch? Come around in front of us or I'll kill your friend."

"Willy's not really my friend," said Chad. "We just work together. Right, Willy? Besides, I have a stunner snuggled up to your boy's left ear. And I'll kill him, if you don't drop yours."

"We're at an impasse, then." Indigo sounded very calm. "Because you need to know that if you kill that boy, I'll turn this stunner on myself." Indigo brought the stunner Willy had kicked to him out of his pocket. He placed it to his own throat, while keeping the first stunner pointed at Willy, and turned around to look at the man. "I don't think the people at the Ganivar station will be too happy if you end up with two dead subjects, will they?"

"He's right, Chad, they said they want them alive! So they can study 'em."

Chad sighed. "Thanks, Willy."

"I suggest a trade," said Indigo.

"No." Pathik spoke softly. His eyes pleaded with his grandfather.

Chad's grip on Pathik's shoulder tightened and he shoved the stunner tighter against Pathik's head. "I'm listening."

"Let the boy go." Indigo smiled at Chad. "Then we'll sit down together and wait, until the sun has set." Indigo shifted his gaze to Pathik, and made certain he was listening carefully. "Once the sun has set, you can free your colleagues, and you can call your superiors and let them know you have one of the leaders of the Others. They will want me much more than they would want this boy."

"It makes no difference which one of you we deliver," said Chad.

"But you need to deliver one. And you won't if you don't listen to me now."

Without warning Indigo lunged at Chad, and grabbed Pathik. He held the stunner he had at Pathik's throat.

"Are you crazy?" Chad staggered back.

"I can kill the boy and myself in less than three seconds. Do you want one, or none?"

Chad stared at Indigo for what seemed like a full minute. Finally, he spoke.

"Willy, get in the cell."

Willy didn't hesitate. Chad kept his eyes on Indigo. "I'll take the boy out front and make sure the coast is clear."

Indigo smiled and shook his head. He walked with Pathik to the door, still holding the stunner at the boy's throat. "He can find his own way."

"Grandfather." Pathik whispered the word. Indigo was thankful he couldn't see his grandson's face.

"You must go." Indigo hugged Pathik hard. "Know that I love you always." He whispered into Pathik's ear, never taking his eyes from Chad. "Go as soon as you get back. Don't wait for the sun to set." Then he pushed Pathik through the door. He turned to face Chad, pointing one of his stunners at him. He placed the other against his own throat. "Now we wait."

* * *

JONATHAN HADN'T TAKEN his eyes off the door. It seemed like it had been a long time, and he was pretty certain nothing good was going to happen. He figured he would wait for a while longer, before he headed back to The Property. Then the door opened. The boy stepped out, looked both ways to see if anyone was coming. Jonathan saw him notice the truck. He saw him put his hands in his pockets and start walking. When he reached the truck he opened the door and got in without saying a word. He was crying silently, his cheeks wet with tears. He tried to speak, but he sobbed, once, instead.

Jonathan started the truck. "Are we going?"

Pathik nodded.

They drove away.

CHAPTER 21

"THEY'RE HERE!" RACHEL had been watching from the front door since Jonathan and Indigo left. The others had been busy packing all they could into canvas duffels Jonathan had purchased in Bensen. He had managed to get the medicines he had gone for, but nothing else. He had just been dropping off the duffels and medicines at his truck before going to get other supplies when he found Rachel there. Still, there was plenty in Ms. Moore's house that they felt would be useful. She had only sent a fraction of the things with Rachel that she had been stockpiling in the cellar; there were lots of dehydrated food packs and thermal blankets and other items. And this time there would be many people to carry things, not just Rachel.

"They're here!" Rachel called out again, louder. Ms. Moore heard her from the parlor, and hurried to the door. She stood behind Rachel, hands on Rachel's shoulders, and they watched as the truck came up the long driveway.

"Thank goodness," breathed Ms. Moore.

Rachel squinted. It looked like there were only two people in the truck.

"What . . ." Ms. Moore saw the same thing.

"The back," said Rachel. "One of them must be in the back, under the tarp."

"Of course!" Ms. Moore sounded as relieved as Rachel felt.

The truck pulled up close to the porch and stopped. Jonathan got out of the driver's side. He walked around to the passenger's side and opened the door. Rachel and Ms. Moore could see him speaking to Pathik, who then got out of the truck. Jonathan put an arm around Pathik's shoulders and the two began to walk toward the house.

Rachel felt Ms. Moore's hands leave her shoulders. She heard her footsteps walk away. But Rachel didn't turn around. She couldn't take her eyes off the truck.

When Jonathan and Pathik reached the door, Rachel saw all she needed to know in their faces. She took hold of Pathik's hand. She turned to Jonathan.

"She's gone to the greenhouse, I think." Then she led Pathik upstairs to clean his bloody face.

In the bathroom, he didn't say anything. He just sat, trembling in the oddest way, as though he were cold, while Rachel filled the sink with hot water. He wouldn't look at her, though he winced when she cleaned the cuts on his face.

"Thank you, Pathik." She whispered the words. "For saving me."

He looked at her, so much pain in his eyes that she

gasped. "I put you there. In danger." He looked away. "And him too."

"It was just a mistake—"

"It was stupid."

"If you're to blame, then so am I, just as much."

He looked back at her, angry. "Maybe so." Then he got up and left. She heard him open the door to one of the bedrooms, heard it close behind him.

Rachel stared at the wet cloth in her hand, at Pathik's blood, patterning it with blurry smudges. She sat like that for a long time, before she cleaned up the sink and went downstairs.

THEY WERE READY to Cross. Five duffels sat by the greenhouse door, where they had moved all of the supplies they were taking. Rachel stared at them. She knew what the number meant, though nobody had said anything to her about it.

She heard a noise and looked around. Ms. Moore was still in the back of the greenhouse, where she had retreated once she saw Indigo wasn't in Jonathan's truck. Rachel knew Jonathan had come out to tell her what happened. Vivian had come to talk with her too, and then Daniel, while Rachel and Fisher and Pathik finished the packing. None of them could convince her to Cross.

Rachel walked back toward her. She was putting some orchid starts in clear plastic cubes. She looked up as Rachel approached.

"I want you to take these, Rachel. They're your crosses. If you let them have a little light each day, they should be fine until you get to camp."

Rachel said nothing. She went to the bench and took a plant out of its pot. She watched what Ms. Moore was doing.

"Fill the reservoir with water, see?" Ms. Moore showed Rachel a tiny pocket inside the plastic cube she was holding. "They won't be in great shape, but they'll survive."

Rachel put her orchid in a cube like Ms. Moore had done.

"You won't come with us?" She was careful not to look at Ms. Moore.

"No." Ms. Moore spoke firmly. "I'll wait here. Just in case."

"Jonathan is going to stay too."

"Old fool." Ms. Moore shook her head. "I told him to go, but he says he's too set in his ways. I suppose I should be grateful."

"I'm so sorry." Rachel couldn't hold back her emotions anymore. She had to speak the truth to somebody. "It's my fault about Indigo."

"Rachel." Ms. Moore waited until Rachel looked at her. "Indigo did what he had to do. It's no more your fault that he had to do it than it is your fault that man attacked you in town. Indigo may . . ." Ms. Moore's voice broke, and she had to stop. She took a breath and continued. "He may be fine. He might find a way out. He might not. But I'm not leaving here without him." She reached up and smoothed her hair back into its steel-plated bun. "Now, dry your eyes and help me get these orchids cubed up. You're Crossing in less than an hour." She looked back down at the orchid she was packing.

Rachel watched Ms. Moore's face. If she did believe that Indigo might be fine, it was not reflected there. Rachel bowed her head and got back to work.

LATER, ELIZABETH WATCHED the shadows encroach on the corners of the room. She had sent Jonathan home; better for things to be as normal as possible to any observers of their patterns. The house was silent. They had all gone, and were now on their way to places she would never see. She turned the ring that hung from a chain around her neck— turned it absently in her fingers. She was back to it being her only reminder of love.

She knew he was dead. Or if not, that he would be soon. Before he had gone into town, he had taken her aside. When he looked at her she knew what he had in mind; some sort of swap, him for their grandson. And she approved.

"You'll try, though, to come back?" She hadn't wanted him to just give up.

"Of course." He had smiled at her tenderly. "Do you think I want to miss our chance?"

She sighed. Their chance. She was the one who had ruined that, all those years ago, with her indecision and fear. But she couldn't change it now. She couldn't do anything to change it now. So she sat in her chair, and thought about climbing the stairs to her bedroom.

CHAPTER 22

By the third day they were all exhausted. Vivian had not done anything as physically demanding as trekking through the wilderness for many years, and the rest of them had had only one night's real rest from the trip to The Property before turning around and heading back.

They risked small fires at night, and kept two people on watch at once. Nobody mentioned the baern attack, but everyone was thinking about it. Pathik wasn't talking much to anyone, and that worried Rachel. He said only what was required, and whenever he saw her coming his way he found some reason to move. She saw Daniel take him aside and talk to him, but Pathik seemed unmoved by whatever he had said.

She missed him. And she knew he had to be hurting. She gave him some time, but finally, she waited until he had his back to her and approached him. He was busy with the fire, and he didn't see her until she was right behind him.

He turned to face her as though she were something dangerous.

"You all right?" She took his hand in hers without thinking.

He pulled away roughly. "I'm fine." For a moment it seemed like he would say more, but he just looked at her with eyes she couldn't read, and walked away into the dusk.

Rachel walked away too, numb. She kept thinking about how it was her fault. If she hadn't let Pathik go to town, if that man hadn't grabbed her. She kept seeing Indigo, driving away with Jonathan in the truck.

"Shall we see about gathering some more wood for the fire, Rachel?" Vivian was trying her best to be useful. She wiped her forehead with the back of her hand, and left a smudge of dirt on her temple.

"Sure." Rachel answered listlessly, still thinking about Indigo.

"Oh, Rachel. You've got to snap out of this. It isn't good for you at all."

Rachel shook her head. "How can I? How can I just snap out of it? It's my fault they got Indigo. It's my fault that we're all here in the middle of nowhere, going to who knows where. It's all my fault."

Vivian pulled Rachel toward her and wrapped her arms around her. "It's your fault your father's here with us. It's your fault we are together. It's your fault that Elizabeth was able to see Indigo again, that they were able to know that their love for each other was still there, still strong. It's your fault she got to meet her grandson." Vivian squeezed her, hard. She whispered in her ear. "If you want to blame yourself, Rachel, blame yourself for those things, those wonderful things. None of them would have happened without you." She leaned back so she could see Rachel's eyes. "Life is filled with risk, Rachel. And you have to take it. You taught me that." Vivian smiled and smoothed Rachel's hair. "Now let's go get some wood. I'm ready for dinner."

On the last night before they got back to camp, Rachel found Pathik sitting by himself. He'd seemed to improve slowly over the last few days, talking more, seeming more like himself. But Rachel was still worried. She sat down next to him.

"Pathik," Rachel stammered. She wasn't sure what to say.

He turned to her. "Rachel." He watched to see what she might do, his eyes locked on hers.

She sat, silent, for the longest time. She looked back at him and thought about how he could choose to shrink from love, when he'd seen so much loss. She thought about how she had been shrinking from love, all of her life, how she'd been glad to live on The Property, isolated, with no temptation to make a friend her age, or fall in love. Finally she reached out and took his hand. This time, he let her. This time, he covered her hand with both of his, and when he looked at her, the message in his eyes was clear.

"I'm here," she said. And they sat, close, until it was time to go to sleep.

CHAPTER 23

He's Alive. So we'll have to go get him." Malgam sounded resolute.

Rachel had seen his face when their party straggled into camp. She had watched him as he realized that Indigo was not among them. Seeing the last shred of his hope fade had been a terrible thing.

Daniel shook his head. "How would we Cross, Malgam? Besides, they've taken him to Ganivar by now. There's no way to know where. But wherever he is, security will be beyond anything we could get through. All we would accomplish would be losing more people."

Malgam bowed his head. Daniel was right.

Malgam knew his father was alive because he had looked, as soon as he saw them come into camp without Indigo. He didn't see the emptiness that represented a person's death; he saw darkness. He thought that Indigo must be drugged, and he felt almost worse about that than if he'd been dead.

* * *

AFTER HE SAW that Nandy was taking care of Pathik, and that everyone else seemed well enough, he walked back to the family hut. He wanted to be alone for a bit before the council meeting.

When he got there he looked again, he sought his father's eyes and saw the same darkness as before. He stretched out on the bed he usually shared with Nandy. Lately, since Rachel had been staying in their hut, the boys had all been bunking together and letting the girls have a bedroom to themselves. He missed the smell of Nandy's skin, next to him at night.

He drew the envelope out of his pocket; he'd carried it with him since Rachel gave it to him. Without looking at it he ripped it open. Inside was a single page. He lifted it up where he could see it.

> *Malgam,*
> *Even the weak and the foolish feel love. They just don't know how to make that matter to someone other than themselves.*
> *I have always loved you. And I am learning to make that count. I hope you can forgive me.*
> *Your mother,*
> *Elizabeth*

Malgam smiled, despite himself. He'd never let Indigo tell him much about his mother; he'd always been more interested in harboring his resentment. He wondered, now, if he would ever know anything about her.

INDIGO OPENED HIS eyes. He was awake again. The room was the same: a bleak, gray cell with a bench inside and a table where his captors talked to him. Or tortured him. They wanted to know what his people could do; they wanted to know where they were, exactly; they wanted to know why the twins had no gifts. Didn't all the Others have powers? What was *his* power?

Indigo smiled. The twins; such a handful, those two boys. Such a wonderful celebration when they were born. The bounty of two healthy babies when even one was a rare miracle. And now they were dead. His captors hadn't said as much, but when he asked to see the twins they refused. When he asked how they knew the twins had no gifts, they didn't meet his eyes. They said they knew, and that was all.

They would break him, soon enough. He was an old man, and tired. He couldn't take much more of their pain. He knew what he had to do, and he knew he had to do it soon; much longer and he would be too weak to stop himself from striking out at his torturers. He'd decided long ago that killing wasn't something he would do, not if he had another choice. And it turned out there was *always* another choice. At least one.

He'd been waiting, hoping he could hold out long enough for Daniel and the rest to reach camp; long enough for his son to hear of his fate and seek his eyes. He wanted to tell him he loved him. One more time.

He took his trekker from his pocket. They hadn't taken it from him; they couldn't see the harm in a piece of string with some knots and beads on it. And there was no harm in it; it was just the way his people tracked the time when they were away from camp on a trek. One bead a day. Indigo remembered showing Pathik how to move a loose bead from one end of the string to the opposite end; how to tie it between two knots to signify the day had ended. He remembered telling him that as long as a bead was still free, anything could happen.

He put the string on the table in front of him. He shaped it, until it made the outline of a heart. Sentimental, but if Malgam was seeing, he would understand Indigo was saying he loved him. He looked at the heart for a long time. Then he picked up the trekker and gathered all the loose beads on it. He held them in his hand and looked at them for a moment. Then he slid them all to the other end of the string. He knotted them off, trapping them there. All the days, over. He stared at the vanquished beads, even though it was hard to look at them. He hoped Malgam was watching. He hoped he wouldn't watch too long.

The door to his cell opened. One of the men came in, holding the black case he had had with him the day before. Indigo knew what was in it.

"So," said the man, "I guess we'll see how resistant you're feeling today, shall we?"

Indigo ignored the man. He closed his eyes and began to

try to picture a tube of liquid, just like the one he had seen when he was a young boy, on another terrible day. But this time, he tried to picture the tube inside his own head. When he saw it, he sighed, relieved. Then he began to scrape at the tube's walls, making them thinner and thinner.

NANDY WAS TENDING to Pathik's rib in the main room when Malgam screamed. She had asked him not to look anymore. She told him it would only bring him pain. But she knew he couldn't stop.

She ran to the bedroom where he had gone to rest, Pathik right behind her. One look at Malgam's face told her everything. She turned to Pathik; he had seen too, though Malgam turned to the wall immediately. She took his hand and led him toward his father. Then she retreated and pulled the cloth across the bedroom doorway.

THE COUNCIL ROOM was packed to capacity. People wanted to know what had happened to Indigo. Rachel sat in the back next to Vivian, listening to the murmur of the crowd. She noticed the Roberts girl, the one she had briefly shared quarters with, standing in the back of the room. She realized she'd never even learned the girl's name. Fisher nodded to her from up front next to Michael. Malgam was nowhere to be seen, and she didn't see Pathik either. Daniel stood at the front of the room.

"Please," he said. The second time he said it the crowd began to quiet.

"I know you all want to hear about Indigo." Daniel held his hand up at the swell of sound from the crowd. "I know. But all I can tell you is that he isn't here. He was captured, and we believe he was taken to a city called Ganivar. We don't know if he is alive or dead right now."

"He's dead." The crowd's gasps turned to whispers as Malgam walked up to the front of the room. His eyes were red, but he looked determined. Pathik came up the aisle behind his father, and stood with him. Daniel took Malgam's hand and whispered something to him. Malgam nodded. Then Daniel stepped over to Pathik and hugged him.

"My father died to protect us." Malgam looked at the people in the crowd. "He died because he was being tortured in order to force him to give information about where we are and what we can do. And he didn't want to do that. So he used his own gift to end his life."

The crowd buzzed louder; only a few knew Indigo had a gift. Even fewer knew what that gift had been. Malgam waited a moment to let the people expend some energy, but then he held up his hand.

"I know Indigo wanted us to seek a better place. And I am going. I invite you all to come. The place is called Salishan. Some of you have heard the stories about it. It's an island, and we can go there, and we can live. Without the threat of the Roberts. Without the threat of the Regs. We can live a better life."

"It's a firetale, no more!" Michael thundered the words from the front row. He stood. "I'm sorry, Malgam, for the death of your father. But Indigo had many dreams that were not realistic." There were some noises of assent from the crowd. "What we need to do is stop the threat of the Roberts. They are our real worry, not the Regs. And now that your father is gone, you need to step into his place and lead us. But lead where we can follow."

Malgam glared. "I've told you many times, Michael, I don't need to lead. Just as my father didn't need to lead. People will do what they wish. And as my father did, I can only try to show our people what is right, and invite them to follow. Here, now, we hate the Regs. And we fear the Roberts. And I see no end to that. If you want to stay, then stay. But I am going to Salishan. I want something better, and I believe it's there."

"We can fight the Roberts!" Michael turned to face the assembly. "We can use our gifts to—"

"To what, Michael?" Malgam spoke quietly, but every person in the room attended his words. "To kill?"

"Sometimes you have to kill, Malgam. The Roberts don't hesitate to kill us." Michael held out his hands.

Malgam shook his head. "Perhaps sometimes," he said, his voice weary, "you do have to kill. I don't know. I *do* know that right now, it doesn't feel like we have to make that choice. We have other choices."

Jab stood. "Would we still have Usage, on the island?"

"Yes, Jab. We will always have Usage. Because we will always need to get better at our gifts."

"Usage isn't just about getting better, though." Jab jutted his chin out.

"No, it's not. It's also about how to use our gifts for the good, Jab. You know that."

Jab sat down. "Just a bunch of rules," he muttered.

Malgam looked across the room, at all the faces he knew so well, at the people he had grown up with, and learned to love. And then he walked back down the aisle and out of the room.

THEY LEFT IN the morning. Nobody else from camp had decided to go. Fisher was there to wish them well. But the rest of the camp kept to their beds.

"You're sure you're not coming?" Rachel was the last to speak to Fisher. She had seen him say his good-byes to the rest of the group. He'd talked a long time with Pathik, and they'd parted with a hug. Rachel wondered what they had said.

He smiled at her. "Not this time. Are you sure you're going?"

She nodded. "You know I am."

"I'll see what I can do here. I think maybe some of them just need time to think about going. Who knows, some of us may show up when you least expect us."

Rachel didn't think they would. She felt like she would never see anyone from the camp again. She thought of Bender, and smiled. She would miss some of the Others.

"Well," she said. "Good-bye, Fisher." And she turned away and began to walk.

CHAPTER 24

THE BOATS WERE there, just as the stories claimed. They were nine days out from camp, out of high tide's way on a wind-scoured beach. There were three, upside-down, metal hulls shining in the midday sun. As they drew nearer, they could see that two of them were ruined; the bottoms were riddled with some sort of bullet holes. The third boat was oddly unharmed.

"Should have hit all three, from the looks of the trajectories." Daniel was examining the bullet holes.

Malgam joined him. "Maybe the third wasn't here when those were shot." He and Daniel exchanged a look. "Wonder where it might have been."

The seaworthy boat was barely big enough for the six of them. When they flipped it over, they found two sets of oars stowed neatly beneath it.

"Let's load it up and get it on the water." Daniel set his duffel inside the boat. Nipper leaped in and settled on a cross board.

The night before they left camp, Rachel had watched the Woolly bump his head against Nandy's hand, asking for attention.

"Will he come?" Rachel had seen how sad Nandy looked as she stroked Nipper.

"He should stay here, where his home is." Nandy frowned.

"But I thought he was yours."

"He's not mine." Nandy scratched Nipper's forehead. "He belongs to his own self. But I will miss him."

In the morning, Nipper had had his own ideas. He followed fast on Nandy's heel and refused to leave her, even when Malgam tried to chase him away. After the third run at him, Malgam had trudged back to Nandy, breathless.

"I think you'll have to let him come, love." And Nandy had called to him, and petted him and laughed. And so Nipper came with them.

Pathik stepped up and put his bags in the boat too. He turned to look at Rachel. For the first time since they had left The Property, he smiled a real smile. Rachel smiled back at him. She looked around at Nandy and Malgam and Vivian and Daniel. Everyone was smiling.

The water was fairly calm right offshore. They strapped everything in and consulted the map and the compass to be certain they knew which direction they should head. Daniel and Malgam took the first stint at rowing. They had about eight hours ahead, if they'd figured correctly.

Rachel watched the shore recede behind them. She didn't feel afraid at all.

That changed.

CHAPTER 25

ELIZABETH WATCHED AS Jonathan walked toward the greenhouse. His image was speckled with smudges and dirt, from the greenhouse glass that hadn't been properly cleaned since Rachel left. Elizabeth didn't care. She didn't care about much now.

"I've made a little something to eat, up at the house." Jonathan still sounded almost shy about his presence in the main house. He'd been staying there since they all Crossed. She wasn't certain if he was worried about EOs coming around or if he thought she would kill herself as soon as he let her out of his sight. He hadn't asked if he could stay; he'd just shown up with an overnight bag the night they left, and moved into the guest room.

"I suppose it's more of your soup?" Elizabeth smiled. He didn't seem to know how to make anything but soup. They'd had endless varieties of it, soup for lunch, soup for dinner. She sipped some to please him, but she wasn't ever hungry.

"I tried something a little different." He turned to go and then turned back. "You coming?"

"I'll be there soon."

The table in the dining room was set for two. He'd tried to put everything in the right place, but he had the water tumblers wrong. It looked like the "something a little different" was sandwiches. She sat while he was still in the kitchen, so that he wouldn't have a chance to fuss at pulling her chair out.

He came out carrying a pitcher of water and a book.

"What's that?"

"This," he said, pouring her water, "is a book from Bensen Library." He sat down at his place.

"It smells quite musty. Do we have to have it at the table while we eat?" She looked at her sandwich with a marked lack of enthusiasm.

"It's a book about that island. The one Rachel said they were going to find."

Elizabeth kept her eyes down.

"At least I think it is." Jonathan flipped the book open to a marked page. "It says here that these islands were excluded from Unifolle's border system—cost too much money, of course. And the big one has to be the one Rachel meant— she said they called it Salishan. Here." He pointed at a map in the book. "It's just called 'relinquished lands,' with a number next to it."

"Why would I care to know this, Jonathan?" Elizabeth had to steel herself not to scream at him to shut up. She didn't want to know about where Rachel was going, about where *she* should have been going, with Indigo. She didn't care.

Jonathan looked up from the book. He watched her for a minute, and then he spoke.

"You don't care now, Elizabeth. But I know you. I know you will care someday. And I think I might be up for a trip, myself. But that trip will take some planning, and some finagling and some work. And I just figured I'd start that going, while you get some rest."

Elizabeth still didn't look up. She thought about how he had seen her through another time like this—a dark time. She thought about how he had tried to keep her here. Now he was ready to help her go. But Indigo was dead. What was there to go for?

As if he had heard her thoughts, Jonathan answered her. "There are lots of different kinds of love, aren't there?"

She looked up at him.

"That girl loves you, Elizabeth. And I know you love her. That's worth going."

Elizabeth looked back down at her sandwich. She still felt numb, and cold, and bleak. But maybe he was right. Maybe she wouldn't feel that way forever.

"Jonathan," she said.

"Yes, Elizabeth."

"I think, tonight, I'll cook."

CHAPTER 26

About four hours into the passage, the skies turned gray. The wind grew chill and the waves grew choppy. They did their best to row, but the boat bucked so hard on the waves that much of the time the oars weren't even in the water. When the rain started coming down in sheets, Rachel didn't see how the storm could get worse.

The storm got worse.

The waves were so big by nightfall that Rachel began to think of them as fluid mountains; they rose up and up and up before the tiny boat, and then crashed down upon it with such force it felt like they would be driven below the sea. Malgam struggled to keep them headed toward shore with the last remaining oar. They were taking on water at such a rate that they couldn't hope to remain afloat for much longer. Pathik and Daniel bailed frantically, but they may as well have been lounging on deck for all the difference their efforts made; the storm was too much. Rachel, Vivian, and

Nandy began to untie the duffels from the boat and tie them all together; they thought if they got washed overboard they might have a better chance of floating ashore in one piece. Rachel grabbed two of the orchid cubes and shoved them deep into her jacket pocket. She tried to bail water with her hands, but she almost fell out of the boat when a big wave hit. Pathik saw and shook his head frantically.

"Just hold on! Hold on to the boat!" He waved his arms so that Vivian and Nandy looked over. "Watch the rhythm!" Rachel could barely hear Pathik's shout over the storm. He pointed to a cresting wave. "Brace yourself when it gets like that. Otherwise you'll be swept away when it comes down."

Rachel grabbed the side and held on. She looked for Vivian and Nandy and saw that they too were readying themselves for the onslaught of the wave. Nandy was holding on to Nipper as tightly as he would let her. Daniel and Pathik kept bailing until the last possible moment, and Malgam kept rowing, but when the wave reached its full height, they too held tight to the nearest part of the boat they could. For a time there was nothing but the water, battering them all, seeking their fingers, loosening their grips.

When it was over, Rachel wiped the seawater from her eyes and tried to see where everyone was. Everyone was still in the boat. She saw that Nandy's head was bowed, and she looked like she was crying, though Rachel couldn't hear over the sounds of the storm. She didn't understand at first, but then she realized Nipper was gone. She turned and leaned over the edge of the boat to see if she could spot him. She couldn't see anything but more waves, at first. But then she saw something . . . at least she thought she did. It was hard to tell with the rocking of the boat, but on the crest of the next wave she was sure. It wasn't the Woolly she saw—it was something else.

"Look! I see it!" Rachel shouted to the others over the sounds of the storm. She pointed at the thin, dark line. It had to be Salishan.

Then she heard Nandy scream. She was pointing too, at the biggest wave Rachel had seen yet. It was high above them, and on its way down. Rachel grabbed for the boat.

When it hit it felt like something solid, like a wall of rock hitting. It knocked Rachel out of the boat as though she were nothing. She flew, over the edge, into the water. And then under.

CHAPTER 27

THE LAST THING Rachel remembered was taking a deep breath, just as she was driven underwater by the waves. Then, nothing. So she didn't understand how she came to be lying on cold, wet sand, coughing up seawater in the dark. But there she was.

She lay, gasping, for some time. She could see a blotchy, starless sky above her, the moon peeking out from behind ragged clouds. She heard the waves washing ashore, felt them touch her legs with clammy fingers. She sat up. And saw Pathik, lying a few feet away.

It didn't look like he was breathing.

"No. No, no," she mumbled, just under her breath. She couldn't stop shaking. She tried to stand, but her legs folded under her. Finally she crawled, scrabbling along until she was next to him. For a moment, she just lay there, aching and tired and weak. She didn't want to take the next step. She didn't want to know the future.

But then she felt his utter stillness. She sat back up and looked at his face, his pale, beautiful face, and then she pushed him over, so he was lying on his side. Water trickled out of his mouth, but he didn't breathe. He didn't breathe. She sobbed, and she hit him, hard, on the back. She hit him again, and again.

And then he coughed.

And then, he *breathed*.

SOMEHOW, THEY ALL made it.

When Pathik gathered enough strength, he and Rachel staggered down the beach, leaning on each other, looking for hope. And they found it, in body after moving, breathing body. Nandy first, crouching in the wet sand, shaking from the cold. Then Daniel, then Vivian and Malgam, helping each other out of the surf. They all laughed and laughed and none of them could stop for a time. Then, they cried.

And then they built a fire.

"It's likely all of it will wash ashore," said Daniel.

They had found one of the duffels; the one Rachel hadn't been able to grab to tie to the others. It contained dry clothes and three foil bags of stew. Daniel had heated the bags and they were all taking turns dipping into the contents with their knives. Everyone had at least one dry item of clothing on, and the rest were quickly drying from the heat of the fire. They tried to scout a bit; they could see dense forest farther inland, and it looked as though there was a mountain range in the far distance. They were too tired to get very far from the beach they washed ashore on.

They didn't find Nipper.

"We'll have to check along the beach in the morning." Vivian looked exhausted, but somehow, she still looked as happy as Rachel had ever seen her.

"I'm for sleeping," said Nandy. She didn't look like she held out much hope for finding Nipper alive. "And I apologize, but I cannot take first watch."

Malgam put his arm around her. "I'm sorry, love. I know what he meant to you."

"I can take first watch," Pathik said, watching his father and Nandy.

"Me too," said Rachel.

They finished the food, and dug out shallow beds in the dry sand. Soon the four adults were asleep. Rachel watched their chests rise and fall, and listened to their snuffling and snoring with quiet joy. She reached out for Pathik's hand. He took hers, and they looked into each other's eyes for the longest time, smiling.

"There doesn't seem to be anybody here," said Rachel. "Or at least, they don't have a late-night welcome crew."

He nodded. "Indigo liked to tell stories. Sometimes, only half of the story was true."

Rachel thought about that.

"But sometimes," said Pathik, "all of it was true."

Rachel nodded, and smiled. She didn't even care if the whole story was true. She was alive and so was Pathik.

"It's a big island," she said. "I guess we'll find out what's true in the morning."

ACKNOWLEDGMENTS:

*Thanks as always to Kirby Kim,
a wonderful agent.*

*And thanks again to all the folks at Dial, including:
Kathy Dawson, Claire Evans, Jenny Kelly, Greg Stadnyk,
Regina Castillo, and Lauri Hornik.*